Cinderella on the Couch

An Inspirational Novel For Those Who
Deserve A Happy Ending

A Novel By

Chris Linnares

KOTOTAMA
PUBLISHING

www.kototamapublishing.com

Submit to Kototama Publishing 101 5th St N. Fargo ND 58102.
Or email at bmarcil@kototamapublishing.com

Library of Congress Cataloging in Publication Data

Library of Congress Control Number: 2007924516

ISBN-13: 978-0-9777371-0-9

Printed at Forum Communications Printing www.forumprinting.com

Book Cover Illustration Matt Mastrud at www.punchgutstudio.com

This book is written for the memory of Maria.
Whose journey taught me one of the biggest lessons in my life.

Never leave for tomorrow the love
I can express today.

Wherever you are, receive my warmest hug.

Acknowledgments

First I would like to express my deep gratitude to God.

And I would like to thank the many people who have made this book possible …

My husband, Billy, for your support, faith, and love, and for giving me the greatest gift of my life, our daughter Luiza.

For Zoë and Isabelle, the best daughters that a stepmom could have.

For my mom who has always believed in me,
even when I didn't believe in myself.

For my father who I love so much and is no longer with us.
Where he is I am sure he is giving me his proud and happy smile
that always had inspired me to be better.

For my brothers and my sister for always being there for me.

Bill and Jane Marcil, whose support has been invaluable in bringing this book to publication.

I want to express my gratitude and respect to the talented professionals who worked with me to edit this book: Tammy Swift, Grace Fraga, Cathy McMullen, Tracy Larson and Carol Leach.

Fernanda Sampaio for the English translation.

Sue Wiger, Marilei Schiavi, Maisa Sabonaro and Ann Rathke who gave their precious time to read the book and give their important additions and comments.

For the talented artist Matt Mastrud for the cover illustration.

Mark Strand for his excellent typography skills.

To all the people who attend my seminars and shows. You help me to share my thoughts, emotions, and become a better person every day.

And a special thanks to you the reader …

You are the main reason for the existence of this book.

For those who deserve a happy ending

Cinderella on the Couch

Table of Contents

Chapter 1

A Life That's No Fairy Tale

Have You Ever Felt Like Life Has KICKED You in The **Gut?**

I have. It was one of the worst times of my life. I felt deceived and rejected after learning my husband, to whom I had dedicated 15 years of my life, left me for a co-worker of his. There I was with three children, one dog, no husband and no work experience. I'd been so involved in raising my family that I'd lost sight of who I was. The pastimes I'd once enjoyed, such as swimming, were suddenly just that – things of the past. At 36, I'd hit rock bottom. First I did what any self-respecting mother of three would do – I panicked. Then, with the support of my friends, I threw myself into what I saw as my only marketable skill – cooking. I started small, preparing and selling frozen gourmet meals. My business grew, and so did my list of customers. Robert, a sophisticated and well-mannered attorney with a large client base and gourmet tastes became a favorite client. Seven years have passed, and I'm now married to Robert. He is my best friend, my husband and my business partner. You can find our products in upscale food stores across the country. I take care of the company, my family, and most importantly myself. I even find time to swim three times a week. I am finally a happy and fulfilled woman!

You have just read Heidi's inspiring story. If you also have a heroine's story to tell, don't waste another minute. Share your special story (500 words maximum) by e-mailing it to Everyday Heroines, care of America's No. 1 women's magazine, Women & Co. ...

... and *blah, blah, blah. Ugh! One more supremely fulfilled woman and I'm going to retch! If I Have to read one more happy ending in this magazine, I may tear out my hair. Why do happy endings always happen to somebody else? Why is life so unfair? It seems every woman I see is flashing a mega-carat ring, while the only ring I have is around my teensy apartment's 40-year-old bathtub.*

How come some people seem to have such fabulous lives while the rest of us keep slogging along with far less than fabulous? Do I sound bitter? Don't answer that.

When I'm feeling particularly cynical, I wonder how many of these "Everyday Heroines" are for real. That's why I like to imagine that behind these outlandish and preposterous "heroines" there's always a crazy and lonely woman. She makes up these stories and sends them to the magazine so she can escape her own mediocre life, which she washes down with pints of Ben & Jerry's Chunky Monkey while comforting herself with empty commitments "to start a new diet on Monday." Oops ... I think I just described me. Talking about me, I might as well mentally replay the familiar short film of my life ...

First Act: Inspiration for my full name – Annie Joseph Sanders. Mom, what were you thinking when you saddled me with that middle name? My mother, the world's most devout Catholic, always gave the same excuse: "I made a promise to St. Joseph for you to be born healthy." I guess it could have been worse. She could have made a promise to St. Luchesius, the saint of lost vocations, to help me find my calling. Annie Luchesius Sanders would have really attracted the prom dates.

I'm single, I work my ass off at something I don't care about, I'm broke, I'm not particularly pretty, and I dream of a life that's a million light-years from my desk. But, hey, I was born healthy. Thanks a lot, St. Joe.

About the single part. It was only three years ago I was destined for married life when I discovered my fiancé was cheating on me. I know it's a cliché, but that didn't keep it from hurting any less. The "happily ever after" I looked forward to was gone in one horrible instant. Since then, I've let the whole notion of marriage and children go the way of other lost causes and focused on my professional life.

My professional life: What can I say? Let's put it this way, it would take more than a patron saint, even Luchesius, to save that one. Don't get me wrong. I believe in a Higher Power, but I don't know if this Higher Power believes in me. I wonder about a God who used creative energy and splendor in building the gorgeous Swiss Alps, the fabulous Grand Canyon and the stunning beaches of Brazil, but who took a few shortcuts when he created his supposedly most amazing creation: me. Seriously, I know in my heart that miracles can happen, even though I never saw the parting of the Red Sea.

Sometimes I ask myself whether God really knows where I live. Does anybody know how I can contact him? Why is it that some people seem to have a direct connection with God, or a Higher Power, or whatever the politically correct term is these days? Do they have a special password? Can I use my PIN number, even if the account is in the red?

Back to my professional life. Women & Co. magazine owns my working soul. Why else would I be subjecting myself to an article like "Everyday Heroines"? I'm not that much of a masochist. Reading it is part of my job. Yes, I'm a frustrated journalist on the editorial staff at Women & Co., the classic example of what I like to call an "estro-zine," a magazine dedicated to helping women "improve" their lives through educating them on everything from their wardrobes to their hairstyles to their orgasms. It's the type of publication that promises to teach female readers how to become geishas in bed, instead of just leaving them alone to have a good, old-fashioned orgasm.

Our demographic – millions of 20- and 30-something, well-educated females – is willingly bombarded with articles such as "If you don't have fun during sex, you're frigid." Or: "If you have too much fun during sex, you're a nymphomaniac." Or: "If your partner knows your G spot, he must also find your H, I and J spots." It's enough to send a girl rushing for Häagen-Dazs.

Which brings me back to my job. I'm in charge of the "Gourmet Delights" section of the magazine. Thank God I'm no longer in charge of "Everyday Heroines," I still have to read it, though, to be "plugged in" to the magazine's greatest hit. Our readers love sagas that clog their brains with the fat of fake reality. OK, so my work clogs their coronary arteries, but hey, at least I make fewer victims. My column is the least-read in the magazine.

So basically I studied my brains out for years, earning my master's degree in journalism at Columbia to write recipes that go unnoticed by women who want to conquer the world but can't turn on a stove. I guess I'm just lucky they haven't decided to cancel me yet. Then where would I work? In the mailroom? That's me: poor journalist diligently working her way down the corporate ladder. I've become one of those people who works just to make ends meet, not to find fulfillment or to make a difference. I'm not sure when this happened … somewhere between the salad course and the entrée.

Do you know what I'd really like to do? Write a book. But in a world filled with bestsellers like "Five Steps to Achieving your Dreams," no one wants to buy a book about a woman who's five million steps away from fulfilling her dreams. My real passion is writing short stories. It's a secret I keep in the vault. But every once in a while, when I'm not too tired and there's nothing good on TV, I'll sit down at my computer and write. It might be a little essay about the lonely old man sitting in the park or that plain-looking young piano teacher I sometimes see in the window of the apartment across from my building. I've been doing it for years.

My stories used to be sad, but lately I've found myself giving them happy endings. The piano teacher falls in love with an adult student. The old man discovers an elderly woman who always sits on a bench on the other side of the park. It's funny how I've found ways to save my characters from loneliness, but I can't figure out how to save myself.

Wait! Hold the movie. God, how did I start thinking about that? I really should be trying to find the damn instructions to my diet. Should I eat lettuce or endives today? Ugh, I think it's watercress. Oh, crap! To make matters worse, here comes obnoxious Ashley the intern to annoy me just because I haven't …

"Annie, two things, honey. Your dad called again, but I know you won't call him back, and second, have you finished the article? Just wanted to give you the heads-up that Paige has been asking that new assistant features editor whether she's seen it."

First: Paige is my boss. Second: Why does Ashley bug me so much? In her own nosy way she's trying to be helpful. Maybe

I resent that she reminds me of how I once was. I used to get super-excited about the office intrigues and assignments too. But that was years ago – before I realized working hard and being nice would just leave me forgotten and shoved aside. On top of that, something happened since I hit my 30s. Must be hormones. I used to get PMS five days a month; now it feels like 25. And I certainly don't want to be reminded of my dad so early in the day. I'm sure Ashley thinks I'm some monster who has pushed him out of my life. If only she knew how much he's hurt me …

"Oh, and Annie, did you hear the news?"

"Hmm?"

"This is big. Paige is going to choose one of the writers for a top investigative story on some secret society that's supposedly changing people's lives. Who knows? Might be you!"

Oh my God, is Ashley for real? A big investigative story? I would never be chosen for something that important. Paige hardly even knows my name.

The only reason I got stuck with Ashley in my already-cramped cubicle is because I rank so low on the food chain. Here I am, a hardworking professional who has to share my workspace – and even my phone – with a know-it-all 22-year-old who is probably salivating over my job. To make matters worse, she always grabs the phone first – partly because she wants to keep tabs on who is calling me. She seems to have appointed herself as poor, pathetic Annie's personal warden. Ugh. If only she were sensitive enough to see I'm having a lousy day.

After those homeless people screaming at each other in the street last night, then the god-awful traffic. God knows how I managed not to scream and flip off every single driver before abandoning my car – right there on the Metro Bridge …

Sharing this tiny and murky (are two functioning fluorescent bulbs really going to bankrupt a multimillion-dollar company?) cubicle with such an exasperating person is not what the Big Guy had in mind when he asked us to "Love thy neighbor." OK, OK. Easy Annie. Take a deep breath and be nice to the cheerleader. She's waiting for me to say something.

"Not to worry. The article's been done for three days, and when Miss Paige asks for my homework assignment, I'll turn it in."

Something about Ashley brings out a sarcastic streak in me. It's not pretty, and I'm not proud of it. I just don't seem to be able to stop it. Thankfully, Ashley doesn't seem to notice.

"I know, but is it the article for this month's issue?"

"Yes, homemade truffles."

"Boy, do I *love* truffles. It must be great being the queen of the food section. I don't mean that you're queen-size. It's just that when you're not eating great food, you're writing about it."

There it is. The look I hate the most. The "do-I-ever-feel-sorry-for-you" look. Unknowingly, she has hit on the main dilemma of a food writer or editor. Fulfilling your job without filling yourself out. I haven't been very successful at that. My longstanding love affair with food, both making and eating it, doesn't help. My mother was a great cook, and baking was her specialty. For as long as I can remember, there we would be, side by side, up to our elbows in cookie dough or whatever. She'd say, "Let's make magic," and together we would whip up something wonderful.

I was stinging from Ashley's remark and from a sense of loss. Ashley, more perceptive than usual, was quick to realize that she had hit a sore spot and changed the subject.

"But really. The grapevine has it that you will be the writer on the undercover assignment on the secret society. I totally believe you can do it. Maybe it's some kind of a Scientology rip-off, or maybe it's the real thing. Say, if you get this assignment, promise me you'll let me in on it. It would be so cool!"

I'm irritated but have to admit I feel grudging admiration. She is so much better at plugging into the office grapevine than I am. Maybe if I actually took the time to talk to some of my co-workers – still, she could just be spreading crazy rumors.

"I've worked here for five years, and I've never been called into Paige's office. If Paige even saw me sitting here, she'd think I was some over-the-hill intern."

"That's terrible. I think you're a great writer. My mom loves your column. Last weekend, she made your recipe for the deep-dish apple-currant pie, and it was yummy."

Oh, great. Found my calling: publishing recipes for Ashley's mom. What a life-altering moment. I turn back to my computer screen and start to type, but Ashley doesn't take the hint.

"I love 'Everyday Heroines.' My favorite is the cleaning woman at the cosmetics company. She must be quite a woman to go from scrubbing floors to marrying the president of the company and founding a charity for sick children all within one year."

Ashley continues to chatter on, but I'm no longer listening. Ben, the gorgeous, "I'm-more-charming-than-Brad-Pitt" advertising director of our companion publication, Men & Co., is strutting around.

This guy thinks he's some hot stuff. And he should. He looks better than the models. The long legs and confident stride of a natural athlete. Tanned skin against the cream collar of an Armani shirt. Thick, longish hair deliberately cut and styled to look as if he just tumbled out of bed and ran his hands through his curly locks. It's no wonder he's gone out with half of the skinny, silicone-packed blondes in the editorial department – and the other half he's rejected. He's good-looking, charming, sexy, great-smelling.

But the practical part of my brain can't keep still. Hello! Wake up, Annie! A man like that wouldn't even look at you. And even if he didn't mistake you for a file cabinet, you wouldn't give him the time of day. You set yourself free from "codependency on men" when you caught him in bed with your maid-of-honor-to-be.

It was the last straw in a long history of being bruised, used and abused by men. Of course, the worst betrayal was by my own father. I haven't seen Dad for years, and I don't care whether I ever see him again. I wonder whether he ever thinks of me? I wonder whether he realizes he's partly responsible for my being alone and miserable and forever distrustful of men? Well, better save that story for Oprah.

The closest contact I allow myself to have with the opposite sex nowadays is with the doorman. Our hands touch ever so lightly when he hands me the mail.

Ashley's chipmunk voice interrupts my thoughts.

"Hey, Annie, honey, don't you think Ben's a hunk?"

"No, I do not."

"Oh, oh, look over there. Gabrielle is talking to him in front of Paige's office."

"Yeah, I see them."

Lord, do I see him. I'm seeing, I'm listening, I'm smelling, I'm drooling. Ben awakens senses I thought were dead and gone. But he's going out with Gabrielle, one of the magazine's perkiest Barbies. She's in a whole different world than I am. Oh no, here comes Ashley, again.

"Annie, honey, miracles do happen. Guess who I heard is being assigned this investigative report?"

I'm laying my bets on Gabrielle, one of Paige's favorites. Still, I feign interest.

"Who? Spit it out, girl. I have to try these new almond cookies and decide whether I'll include them in the next issue."

"You!"

"That's a good one, Ashley. Article by Santa Claus and photos by the Easter Bunny. Come on, be serious."

But little Miss Ashley is practically hyperventilating with excitement.

"It's you, Annie, I swear. Paige's assistant told me but swore me to secrecy."

Yeah, that's like telling Liz Smith to keep a secret.

"That's impossible. Paige doesn't even remember who I am."

"But if she does remember, then this project may be the greatest break of your life."

"I'll believe it when I see it." As if on cue, the phone rings. Ashley grabs for it.

"Hello. Who? Annie *Joseph* Sanders?" She covers the receiver and dramatically stage-whispers, "Joseph?"

I nod, unenthusiastically. Great. How on earth did someone at work get my middle name, even though I never use it? Maybe it's a call from administration or someone who has access to my personnel file. Oh, God, maybe it's H.R. and I'm going to be fired.

"Yes, she's here. All right, I'll give her the message. Bye."

Ashley swivels her chair toward me and cackles with glee.

"Annie, honey, get ready. Paige wants to talk to you. I'll bet you a hundred bucks she's going to give you that secret society assignment."

Me? An investigative reporter? I could see if Paige wanted something top-secret from the food beat, such as "Chipotle Confidential" or "The Day the Shiitake Hit the Fan," but I'm not ready for this. I haven't done any "real" reporting for years. I'll mess it up, like everything else in my life. Now I'm queasy. As I walk toward Paige's office, my feet grow heavier. The worst part is that I have to walk by Ben and Uber-Barbie and watch them flirt. What if all this is Ashley's sick idea of a joke and Paige really wants to fire me? Maybe she is PMS-ing (Prepared to Murder Someone). Maybe she has concluded the best I can contribute to the Women & Co. team is to wash her fine china after one of the fabulous dinner parties she and her fabulous law-partner husband throw every month.

Oh. My. God. I can't believe this. I just bumped into Ben and made him spill coffee on his perfect Armani shirt! Annie Joseph, born healthy and clumsy. So now what? If this were a romantic flick, he would look deeply into my eyes and fall madly in love. But this is my lame excuse for a life, so he'll probably look deeply into my eyes and get me fired.

I try to sputter out an apology.

"I'm so sorry, I didn't …"

Even as I spot Uber-Barbie smirking at me, I can't help but notice his eyes look surprisingly kind.

"Don't worry about it. It was an accident."

"It's just that I was walking and thinking … thinking and walking. I mean, I was doing both at the same time. I can take your shirt to the cleaners if you'd like, sir."

Sir? Where the hell did that come from? He flashes a startling white grin and sticks out a tanned hand.

"Come on, no need for formalities. My name is Ben, and I'll take care of the shirt. Don't worry about it."

"Are you sure? Really? OK, again, I'm so sorry!"

"I've never seen you before. What's your name?"

"Annie Joooooo … Jovial!

Jovial? Jovial?!! What's going to come out of my mouth next? My weight? The day I planned to get my next period? Why did I almost say my middle name? I couldn't help it. I was trying not to tell him my horrid middle name, but I wound up saying something much worse!

"Your name is Annie Jovial?"

"I mean, I-I'm the jovial Annie"

I stammer, hoping he can tell the difference between me and the magazine's "other" Annie – an ancient, cantankerous woman who works in the fact-checking department and smells like cat litter.

"OK, well, anyway, bye. Gotta go. Again, sorry!"

He rewards me with another toothpaste-ad grin.

"Jovial Annie. She is funny. I never saw her in the department before …"

It's the last thing I hear Ben say to Uber-Barbie, who must be laughing herself silly. "Funny," he called me. Which probably means "funny – like a circus freak." Still, I can't help but notice what a piercing look he gave me. Is it even remotely possible? Nah, forget it. Focus on the mission at hand.

Still shaken, I reach Paige's open door and knock lightly. She glances up from her paperwork and then nimbly removes her chic Gucci eyewear.

"Good morning, Annie. Please, sit down. Is everything all right with you?"

"Yes, thanks, Paige."

Look at this woman. From her Prada stilettos to her exquisitely pinstriped Chanel suit, she is elegance personified. Oh to be at the helm of one of the country's hottest women's magazines. (God, could it really be me thinking this – the frumpy food writer who apparently has been brainwashed by all those nights alone watching "Queer Eye" and "Project Runway"?) But who could resist the possibilities of such a life? Travel abroad every year with nanny and picture-perfect family in tow, Louis Vuitton luggage packed with the latest designer fashions, Jimmy Choos for every occasion and cellulite cream made from the sweat of an ovulating African ostrich (although I seriously doubt Paige would suffer from such a mundane flaw as thigh dimples).

"I'll get straight to the point, Annie. We have no time to lose. I'm going to assign you an investigative piece. It's very important. You've been working with us for some time. What is it? Two years?"

"Actually, five."

"That's right, five years. Well, I've decided to assign you an investigative piece, a plum assignment really. As you know, we've been receiving letter after letter to 'Everyday Heroines' lauding the results of a secret group."

"Like what?"

"We can't get a line on that. But what we do know is that people, let's say brokenhearted people, are finding a new peace and happiness. Likewise, people frustrated at work are finding new meaning in their current jobs or the motivation to go out and seek different work. In short, whatever it is that people dare to dream, they are finding ways to fulfill those dreams."

"Do you think there is any truth in the stories? It sounds kind of cultish to me. And the people sound a little bit like losers."

"That's why you're here. I am giving this assignment to you. You are bright and inquisitive, and you are just skeptical enough not to be hoodwinked by some weird, fly-by-night operation. I want you to join and infiltrate the group. Find out how this group is changing lives through fairy tales."

"Fairy tales? Can't they even escape being appropriated by the self-help gurus?"

"Perhaps not. In any case, a new session of lectures is about to begin. On the Cinderella story. Can you imagine that? It seems an awfully big leap to say that this tale is transforming lives."

I agree. A pumpkin turning into a carriage and then back again? A scouring girl turned princess and back again, only to be saved by her Prince Charming and taken back to his castle where they live happily ever after? What does an imaginary character have to teach a generation of women who stopped embroidering their ball gowns long ago and chose to burn their bras instead?

"I'm sorry, Paige, but I can't swallow any of this. We're talking about a children's story here. My guess is that this is a group of frustrated people who can't find happiness on their own, so they turn to some so-called experts who dupe them out of their time and money."

"Annie, I don't know the answers to all these questions. That's exactly why I chose you to be in charge of this report."

"And what exactly am I supposed to do? What do you have in mind?"

"Become a member, get to know their teachings, and write a story on the experience. This is how it works: They don't advertise, so you need to be introduced by a group member. We already have that lined up. I'll give you the address and the time for the meeting, OK?"

"But Paige, what about the risks of going undercover? Do you really think it would be ethical to send me into this group as a 'client' rather than a reporter?"

"We've decided it's our only way to get inside the society. You realize, of course, that we do such stories only as a last resort. Gabrielle actually tried to get an interview with the group last year, but they refused to speak to a reporter. Not only that, there is no 'official' spokesman for the group. They claim they are a grass-roots group that just wants to help others."

"But do we have to pay for this? How does it work?"

"It is a non-profit organization. We know they donate to a few charities and they'll take your donation. That's your way in. They meet once a month."

"When does the next series of meetings begin?"

"Next Thursday."

Yikes, so soon. Thank goodness for my perennially empty social calendar.

"Next Thursday? OK. But what about my section?"

"We're changing it to nutrition. Paula from proofing will be taking over. Our latest readership surveys show our subscribers don't really want to know how many cups of sugar they need to make a chocolate cake. What they do want to know is how to count carbs in the "sugar-free-reduced-fat-tofu-gluten-free-torte-that-tastes-like-chocolate-cake." From now on, we'll publish just one of your recipes so you won't have to worry about writing the entire column. Are you in?"

"Absolutely. It's going to be great."

Or, I'm going to get fired. And I better do a damn good job on this project. Ten years ago it was hard to get a job if you were over 55. Nowadays it's hard enough at 35. Still, I have to admit feeling a twinge of excitement. Yes, I'm afraid I might screw it up, but I'm also kind of eager to prove I can do more than write about crème brulée. Maybe Paige really has been noticing my hard work. Maybe this could lead to other big investigative pieces. Heck, I might even get a raise.

"May I ask you a question, Paige? I'm sure anybody on the staff would kill for this assignment. Why me?"

"Of course we trust you and know you're going to do a good job. Also, we understand that the people who attend these meetings are – how shall I put it? – a little less worldly and are looking for ways to improve their lives. I believe your presence in those meeting won't raise any red flags – you know – you fit their profile so well. I couldn't send someone like Gabrielle there."

"Of course. Well, thanks, Paige. I understand."

Aha! The truth comes out: I'm a nobody, a loser whose nondescript profile is custom-made for the job. Oh, well. No time to dwell on it. I'd better get back to my desk and start digging up background. If these fairy-tale people won't talk to reporters and this is the first I've heard of them, they've probably had little media coverage. Does a "secret society" without an official name even have a Web site? Maybe I should Google for the phrase, "lonesome losers who try to transform life through fairy tales." Oh, great. Ashley is already heading in my direction.

"Annie, honey! How was the meeting? Oh, and before I forget, your father called again. Honey, I've been here for over a year and I can't help but notice you never return your father's calls."

"And I won't return this one either."

"I don't think your mother would like that at all."

"Ashley, honey, first of all: my mother passed away four years ago. Since then, I've lived by myself, carried on with my life and never had to ask for anyone's permission for anything. I haven't talked to my dad for the last seven years. Second: I need a minute to take a breath and take in what's happened to me in the last ten seconds. So, for the first time since we've been sharing an office, could you just give me a minute?"

Ashley actually looks stunned.

"I'm sorry about your mom! I had no idea – sorry if I was intrusive. Are you going to do the special report?"

"Yes, I am."

"When do you start?"

"Next Thursday."

What a mess I've gotten myself into. But refusing the offer would only have meant immediate unemployment. Besides, who knows? What if this is a blessing in disguise? Oh, come on, Annie, you know better than that. You don't have that kind of luck. This is just a job that the managing editor assigned to you because you are a "plain Jane." Not to mention your amazing ability to say yes when you actually are terrified and just want to say no. Meeting with Cinderella. Totally crazy.

Chapter 2

Do I "Empower" Myself?

It's *7:45 p.m. and I'm maneuvering my beat-up Beetle into a parking spot by the building where this alleged "secret organization" meets. The place is much nicer than I thought. Is this the right address? The number's correct and so is the street. Surprise, surprise: There's no sign at the entrance. Even if it weren't a secret group, what would they name it? Fairy Tale Association? League of Extraordinary Lunatics? Losers Anonymous? And look at this parking lot filled with Saabs and late-model SUV's. My little piece of junk is going to get a complex. The house is gorgeous, with flowers and impeccable landscaping. I wonder whether Alice in Wonderland inspired these people? Ha, ha, ha. Just a joke – my little attempt to calm my nerves. Wow, they even have a receptionist. How smart. These people are connected – probably with the Mob.*

"Good evening and welcome, dear. What's your name?"

The elderly woman at the registration desk smiles, looking up through trifocals.

"Annie ... Joseph ... Sanders."

Ugh. Suddenly I can't stop spilling out my middle name to total strangers.

"Well, that's a different name, very strong."

Is she being sarcastic? We're definitely starting on the wrong foot.

"Why don't you come in and join us? You can sit anywhere you'd like. The meeting starts at 8 sharp. Cathy will be right with you so we can get started."

"Cathy?"

"Yes. She'll be lecturing on the inner truths of the Cinderella myth. Last week we finished the Sleeping Beauty series with Grayson, so now it's Cathy's turn."

Funny thing is, this woman takes it so seriously. Hello, lady? It's not like we're studying Plato.

"Do men attend the meetings?"

"Oh, dear, not only do they come to the meetings, some of them can't stop talking about their lives."

This was a surprise. What's any self-respecting man doing at a fairy tale seminar? Maybe they were trying to pick up chicks. Or maybe they are acting out a repressed dream of dressing up as Cinderella.

The meeting room is set up theater style, with a podium in the front. The seating is comfortable and U-shaped. There is an effort to give it an intimate feel even for as large a room as this. The suggestion of intimacy is making me feel nervous, not reassured in the least. I think about escape and remember that a lot is on the line here, including my job, my meal ticket.

I look around for a friendly face, but not one that is too friendly. The last thing I want is to get stuck sitting by somebody who really wants to talk. Sitting next to a talker on an airplane is my idea of slow torture.

Yuck, I hate this. I feel like everyone's looking at me, thinking: "Oh, good. Another sucker." I already feel like a loser. I don't need to add to that. Speaking of losers, everybody here looks pretty normal. Again, I'm not sure what I expected. I guess a loser, like most things, is in the eye of the beholder. I hone in on a woman who looks to be in her 60's. Nicely dressed, pleasant looking, keeping to herself. I have my seatmate.

"Is this seat taken?"

"No, please sit down. I'm Elizabeth, but everyone calls me Liz."

"I'm Annie."

"I noticed you as soon as you came into the room. You remind me much of my daughter. I haven't seen her in 15 years. I miss her terribly."

Interestingly enough, she reminds me of my late Grandma Jane. She was very special to me, and I think of her often. But I know if I tell her that, I'll soon regret it. She'll probably start dumping her life story on me.

"But I'm not going to complain. Because, you know, when we complain, we attract bad vibes. I prefer to focus on the thought that one day I may see my daughter again and give her a great big hug."

The reporter in me never rests. I'm actually thinking this story could have some magazine potential: "Sweet old lady looks for long-estranged daughter."

"Is your daughter missing?"

"It's a long story,"

Please, little lady, give me the Cliff's Notes version. I already have to put up with Ashley all day. I guess I should give her a break; at least she's trying to be nice. Maybe I get that vibe from her because she reminds me so much of Jane.

"Natalie fell in love with an older man. He was 20 years her senior. My husband was still alive at the time, and he was concerned so he told her she couldn't see this man anymore. Women of my generation are different from yours, dear, so I didn't say anything. One night, Natalie woke me. She was crying and begging me to help her. I told her I couldn't go up against her father. She took this as me being against her. I was between a rock and a hard place, but I knew that ultimatums were not a good tactic with such a stubborn girl.

"The next day, I woke to find a note on the kitchen table. Natalie had left. When my husband passed away, I hired a private investigator to find her. He didn't have much luck. Then one day, out of the blue, she sent me a letter. She was in Los Angeles.

"The letter told me that she was really sorry about the worry she caused, but she didn't want to see me because she felt I hadn't been there for her when she needed me most. She said she had two children and she was doing well. I tried to find her, but she had moved. When you came into the room, my heart stopped. For a split second I thought you were her. You have the same beautiful brunette hair and intelligent eyes, just like my Natalie."

This lady is either blind or senile.

"What a story! You don't know anyone who can help you find your daughter?"

"No, I'm living with my sister. She's not very supportive. She says when Natalie wants to, she will know where to find me. Donna's never had children, so obviously she doesn't understand how painful all this is for me. I only want to hug my daughter one more time."

Weird. This lady's sob story actually touches my heart. There, Annie, stop getting involved with strangers or you'll be getting into another mess.

"Have you tried any of those TV programs that help you find lost relatives?"

"Absolutely. I've sent several letters, but never received a reply. My neighbor gave me an idea though. She said those TV reporters can be very determined. They almost always find the people they're looking for."

"That's very true."

"Are you a journalist?"

My heart skips a beat. Where on earth did she get that idea? Great, my cover is blown even before the seminar starts.

"Oh, no, no. I work with computers. I write for a few Web sites. But I know a lot of reporters. Your neighbor is absolutely right."

Liz's face lights up.

"Who knows, dear? If it's not too much trouble, could you maybe ask one of your journalist friends to help me? I have her old address on the letter. It's a start. I also have her married name."

"I can see what I can do for you, but I really can't promise anything."

"And you, my dear, are you close with your parents?"

"Well, my mom passed away years ago."

"Oh, I am so sorry. And your father?"

"My dad? Um … we are not close at all."

"That's too bad. That's why you came to this group? To heal your relationship with him? I heard that these meetings help people learn how to forgive and how to build healthy relationships with others."

"No, no. I came here for other reasons and my relationship with my dad is something even Dr. Phil couldn't help. I'm sorry, I don't mean to be rude and please don't take this personally, but I don't like to talk about our relationship."

If this lady wasn't so nice I would be really mad at her. Why is she asking about my father? Why is it that people always expect us to have a good relationship with both of our parents? I had a wonderful relationship with my mom. Isn't that enough? And why do people – even complete strangers – always want to fix everything? Some things can't be fixed. When it comes to my father, I am broken beyond repair. Enough. I promised myself not to think about him anymore. Let me get back to work. I need to quit feeling sorry for myself and start focusing on learning about this self-help mumbo jumbo.

"So, how did you learn about the group, Liz?"

"My cousin's life was transformed by one of these seminars. He's the one who introduced me to the group. One day I'll tell you all about it. Oh look, Cathy is here. It must be time to start."

A voice, low and smooth, fills the room.

"Hello and welcome to our group. For those of you who don't know me, my name is Cathy. I hope to see you all here once a month for the next five months."

Cathy has really got it together. She must be about 50, but it's hard to tell with that fit body and peachy skin. She's either really health-conscious or she's worried her husband will trade her in for two 25-year-olds.

"During the course of the seminar, we'll sink our teeth into the fabulous tale of Cinderella and try to gain insights to help us improve our own lives."

This is so silly. My cousin's 6-year-old girl would love to be here. But at least Cathy is making an effort to be pleasant.

"I'm sure some of you are asking yourselves: "Why fairy tales? That's for kids. What are we, as adults, going to learn from them? How can they change our lives?"

Cathy asks all the right questions. But does she have the answers?

"Before we start, let's get one thing straight: Fairy tales were not originally written for children. In the old days, adults watched fairy tales, which were performed both at elegant salons and in suburban circles. Fairy tales were derived from popular stories of the oral tradition that were passed from generation to generation. Did you know there's evidence that the story of Cinderella was popular in China in the 9th century?"

OK, at least the woman seems to have done her homework. She even looks like she might be an interesting person. Lively, cheerful, even believable. In other words, another alienated lunatic. Poor thing, it's not her fault.

"Just to give you an idea, one of the first Cinderella stories we know of was called *Yeh-hsien*. Tuan Ch'engshih recorded her story around 850 A.D. Like the Western Cinderella, Yeh-hsien is kind, does the housework and is humiliated by her stepmother and stepsister. In the Eastern version, her salvation appears in the form of a large fish that gives her gold, pearls, dresses and food as gifts. There are several other versions of the original *Aschenputtel* by the Grimm brothers, like *Cendrillon* by Perrault, and the Cinderella story our mothers used to read to us."

Interesting. I'll have to remember to do some homework on the Cinderella myth tomorrow. I had no idea every culture had a version of this story. I guess women from all over the globe fantasize about going to fancy balls and being saved by a dashing prince. Blame it on our mothers for telling us we could live happily ever after. Still, I'm not entirely sure what all this has to do with real life. And now my stomach is growling. I should have had more than a Diet Coke and half a bag of Doritos for dinner. Hey, I have two almond cookies in my bag. Damn. Can't eat them now – too noisy. I hope we have a break … soon.

"I'm sure you are still asking yourselves how fairy tales can help you. Myths are nothing but a reflection of humanity's unconscious mind across time. We inherit different stories from our culture, including fairy tales. Every story, with its nuances, can bring peace to our restlessness and solutions to our problems. In his book, 'The Return of the Goddess,' Edward Whitmont says 'both adults and children are fascinated by fairy tales because it's in fantasy that the human soul experiences its own reality.' "

Hmmm, I'll have to check out this Edward Whitmont book, too. This could really help out my story.

"Please feel free to interrupt if you have any questions. Together we'll start the fascinating journey toward the biggest makeover of your lives. I want to make it clear that nothing I say is the absolute truth. I'll give you my point of view on Cinderella's story and tell you how it transformed my own life."

My original plan had been to stay as inconspicuous as possible, but I can't keep still another minute.

"Excuse me, Cathy. I guess I'm still not very clear on how these stories will help us transform our lives. Transform them into what?"

Cathy looks frankly delighted to be interrupted.

"Good question. What is your name?"

"Annie."

"Annie, when you were a child, what was your favorite fairy tale?"

Oh, come on. She's obviously answering my question with a question because she doesn't have an answer. She's nothing but a quack. But I'd better think of something. Let's see ... Sleeping Beauty? But if I say that, she'll probably psychoanalyze me and say I am a lazy bum who does nothing but sleep and wait for her savior. Maybe Alice in Wonderland? But then everyone will see me as a rebellious child. Seeing my bewildered look, Cathy smiles kindly.

"You don't have to answer my question, Annie. I only want to make everyone here think about this. What fairy tale caught your attention as a child and why?"

Whew, saved by the bell.

"Fairy tales can bring our key dilemmas to the surface and show us ways to solve them. Fairy tales are vehicles for self-knowledge because they put us in touch with our dreams, our conflicts, and our fantasies. The way we deal with our inner world, or our soul if you like, has a strong impact on what we achieve in the outer world. Let's go back to your question, Annie. 'How can these stories transform someone's life?' I want to make one thing clear: No fairy godmother will make your life better. There's only one person who can do that: you."

There's a new shrink in town, and she can spout pop-psychology with the best of them.

"In these meetings, we'll share the teachings contained in Cinderella's story so that you may put them to practice and be more in touch with your inner self. The more you're in touch with your inner self, the more you can improve the world around you."

A pale, paunchy guy dressed in a wrinkled oxford shirt suddenly stands up.

"I'm sorry to interrupt, Cathy. My name is Steve. Could you expand on this "relationship with the inner self?" Isn't this point of view too subjective?"

I'm not the only thinking human being in the place. You go, Steve! I want to see Miss Chatty Cathy talk her way out of this one.

"I love your question, Steve. See, we live in two worlds: the external and the internal. The external world is visible; it is objective. The internal world is invisible and subjective. We process the external world through the five senses. We all share this world. The internal world, the inner self – which includes your thoughts, your feelings and your beliefs – belongs to you alone. We live in this world. We can't get away from it. It's in this world that we feel, suffer and determine our actions. And since our actions directly influence our external world, when we learn to relate to our internal world in a constructive way, then we can say that we have the foundation for a true transformation of our life."

Steve looks as irritated as I feel.

"But how can we relate to our internal world in a healthy way? How can we do that? And what does the fairy tale of Cinderella have to do with all this?"

I'm going to give this Steve guy a kiss and; oh, god, I'm so hungry. I'm this close to going ahead and opening the almond cookies. I can practically hear them calling me. Once again, Cathy seems undaunted, even delighted, at Steve's skepticism.

"The basic plots of fairy tales chronicle the obstacles, or the trials, we need to overcome in life. It's like the ceremonial initiation of a hero's journey toward existential self-realization. In Cinderella's case, the meeting with the prince symbolizes the ideal ultimate goal. We need to know all about Cinderella: her actions, her attitude and the path she took to reach her goal. Buddhism uses the eisho funi principle to explain the close relationship human beings have with their environment. In order to transform your external world, you have to stir a transformation in your internal world. Why? Simply because one world reflects the other.

"So basically, Steve, what we do in these meetings is help you relate to your internal world as a true hero. We want all of you to become heroes and heroines so that you can cause a real transformation in your life. Now, you need to ask yourselves: How am I handling my life trials? Do I really feel fulfilled? Or do I procrastinate when it comes to solving my problems? Have I reached my goals? Do I know what my goals and dreams are? Do I believe I can fulfill them? Or did I give up on them because I thought my dreams could come true only in fairy tales?"

Hold it right there. Houston, we have a problem! I'm completely lost here. Cinderella is no heroine. She's just some spineless bimbo who was blessed with a fairy godmother and a great face. What does some imaginary princess have to teach me about life? Wake up, Steve. Didn't you see that one coming?

Obviously, he did.

"Sorry for interrupting again."

"That's OK, Steve."

"What specific teachings within the Cinderella tale can help me become – for lack of a better word – a hero in my life? I mean, I'm not really waiting for a handsome prince."

He turns and smirks at the sprinkle of giggles rippling through the crowd. All right, my boy. I adore this guy. It's like he can read my mind. If I didn't fear calling undue attention to myself, I'd stand on my chair and chant: "Steve-o! Steve-o! Steve-o!" Uh oh, blood sugar drop – can't focus – I'm so hungry I'm getting sillier than this Cathy broad."

"As I told you earlier, the teachings will be revealed during the meetings. Now I'm aware there's an important issue to be addressed right away. Many people don't see Cinderella as a heroine, rather as a young woman without drive, passively waiting for her savior. Then all of a sudden her life changes magically, and she lives happily ever after. But, as we will see when we re-tell the story, Cinderella didn't really fulfill her life or achieve happiness by magic. If you see it that way, then you are the type of person who thinks victories lie in other people. But if we look at the story under a new light, you may see her differently. What if I tell you the story of a woman who lost her mother, had to work as a maid and be humiliated in her stepmother's home and found success and happiness only after much suffering? Now you can see her as a fighter, can't you? Isn't it worth it to re-examine this story of struggling, suffering, work and fulfillment and see what it has to teach us?"

Steve is obviously not giving up.

"But didn't you say she is a heroine? That this fairy tale is going to help us have a heroic story?"

Steve, will you marry me? It's a shame you're so dorky and I'm so hungry.

"If you look it up in the dictionary, you'll see the words "hero" or "heroine" mean man or woman of extraordinary value. In Cinderella's story, we're going to examine the character's strengths that contributed to her overcoming obstacles and finding fulfillment. And through the practice of these teachings, we are going to re-discover those strengths in each of us so that we can find our own fulfillment and become true heroes – people of extraordinary value."

Great, and where do I buy my Wonder Woman cape? I want to eat, and it looks like we're not going to have a break. Looks like they're not going to serve us anything. Man, even at A.A. you'll get coffee. Cheap loonies.

"So let's start our first activity now. I want to make sure you understand that you don't need to fully believe what I'm saying. Having doubts and asking questions is necessary. You don't even have to believe this is going to change your life. It's key to challenge these teachings. You have to doubt them, but also watch for whatever impact they may have in your life."

That's exactly what I'm going to do, Chatty Cathy. Sorry. I should try to be good and stop making fun of the poor woman's name. If I don't, luck will have it she'll ask me a question. Come to think of it, she may be a bit of a psychic. Better not risk it.

"We are not going to recap Cinderella's story today. First, we have to ask ourselves: 'Do I really empower myself to understand and practice these teachings?' "

God, I can't believe she's dusting off the old dictionary of corporate BS and actually telling me to "empower" myself. Next thing she'll be talking about "synergy" and "thinking outside the box." What does she mean anyway? I'm going to go ahead and ask her. Consider it a shout-out of support to my main man Steve.

"What exactly do you mean by "empower myself'?"

"Let's start with the definition of the word empower, which means to give authority. The word authority means influence, control. Therefore, the question is: Who influenced you to be here today? Who, at this moment, is influencing your life? Is it your friends? Your husband? Your boss? Your parents? I say life, because time is life. The two hours you will spend in this meeting once a month during five months are hours of your life that are being used. And we need to respect our life; it deserves the very best we can do for it. From now on, the basic condition for you to go on attending these meetings is to empower yourselves. Only one person will hold control over that from now on: you. Do you empower yourself to be acquainted with new worlds? Or to look into yourself and rediscover new strengths? Do you empower yourself to truly transform your life?"

Steve, my partner in crime, chimes in.

"If we are here, then it's obvious that we're empowering ourselves."

Steve, you're obviously the smartest man in this room, but you're also the most annoying student ever. Let's run away and get married. But I have to eat first. I should empower myself to eat all the cookies in the world. Speaking of which, I just remembered the time when I was a kid and got really sick from eating a whole bag of Oreos. Who didn't go through that once in their lives?

"Steve, oftentimes we don't empower ourselves to be where we are. We may be influenced by the entire world, everyone except for ourselves. How many people dedicate their lives to a career only to find out later it doesn't fulfill them? How many people feel lonely, try to find someone, and when they do, realize they really want to be alone? And how many people are with someone and decide they want to be alone, only to realize later they want that person back?"

As a matter of fact, the true heroine is Cathy. How can she not blow her top with pesky Steve? It even looks as though she kind of enjoys his questions.

"To illustrate what I just said, I'm going to tell you the story of a woman we'll call Lisa. She pursued a career and wanted to become very successful. The experts said that for her to achieve this, she'd have to give up all aspects of her personal life: love, family, motherhood. Lisa decided a great career was more important, so she didn't waste a minute. She worked very hard – even spending evenings and weekends at the office. Whenever she felt lonely and needed a shoulder to lean on, she remembered what the experts told her: that was for needy people. She needed to cut the cord and find herself, and be detached from everybody else. She had to be strong and independent, to end all co-dependent relationships in her life. She believed and followed this advice. She strived for total independence. And Lisa continued working – living – working. Whenever she needed love, she threw parties, went to expensive spas, attended high-profile movie previews or spent hours at the gym.

"One day, fate knocked at her door. She got married and had a child. They told her motherhood would be a bump in her career and not something she'd cherish. That makes sense, right? A machine doesn't cherish anything. A machine needs to work nonstop, without breakdowns or distractions. So she wasted no time in hiring a nanny for her son and enrolled him in multiple activities. At the end of the day, she kissed him good night and, if she felt something was missing, she reassured herself with magazine articles that declared what was truly important was quality time.

"Lisa stayed in the rat race. Once her son was grown up, the same people who had encouraged her to work and give up the joys of motherhood now accused her of being a bad mother. And Lisa kept on working – and living – and working. She didn't know anything else. Sure, she still feels the occasional empty spot or melancholy. She never looks for a hug or a shoulder to lean on, though, for the same people who encouraged her to give up the joys of motherhood were now encouraging her to take pills that would relieve the anxiety and lessen her depression. And Lisa kept on working."

What a story. I don't know why, but it affects me somehow. Still, I'm not clear on what people made this Lisa woman believe all these things. Was it her mother? Her friends? The media? I guess it doesn't really matter. We women are such suckers. Too often we live our lives according to what other people tell us to do. We're more interested in getting approval than in doing what we really want. How many times have I bought some worthless weight-loss supplements because a buff, washed-up celebrity told me they would change my life? Didn't I once believe my mother when she said getting married and having children would make me happy?

Steve's nasal voice, now dripping with sarcasm, fills the room.

"So, we can wrap up by saying that the best thing Lisa could have done was to take care of her husband and children and abandon her career, right?"

Steve, you're the best. Should we have two children or three? Kevlar Cathy seems impervious to his chiding tone.

"In this story, Lisa let herself be influenced by others to exclude things from her life. She chose. I'll either invest in my career, or I'll invest in my personal life. The biggest challenge of our generation is to learn to trade the 'or' for the 'and' so we can find a sane, balanced way to invest in both our professional and personal lives."

I actually feel a connection with Lisa. I love to be my own boss and have the freedom to do whatever I want. At the same time, I just hate the fact that I can be my own boss and have the freedom to do whatever I want to do.

Finally, another brave soul joins our chorus of fools.

"Hi, Cathy. My name is Karen. I've been coming to these meetings for some time and I really feel a change in my life. I have a question about the story: Who influenced Lisa?"

Alert! Alert! Cult follower in sight! I really should follow this woman and find out whether her life has really improved or she's just another alienated zombie in the Cinder-fool-ya cult. Maybe Cathy pays her to stand up and announce how it helped her.

"Only Lisa can answer that question. Only Lisa could tell you who she empowered to influence her choices. We've all met at least one Lisa in our lives."

Oh, man, this is getting deep. My stomach is roaring so loud I'm surprised it's not drowning out everyone – even Steve. Are we through yet? Cathy again.

"I ask you: Do you give other people power to influence you or not? Are you fulfilled? Are you happy? Do you feel pleasure? Do you allow yourself to feel pleasure? What do you empower yourself for? Do you empower yourself to receive love or do you settle for crumbs? Do you empower yourself to fulfill your dreams or have you forgotten about them? Do you empower yourself to learn teachings that can help you lead a more rewarding life? Or do you still believe that this is nothing but utopia?"

There is total silence in the room. So now I can either dream or unwrap my cookie. I can't even empower myself enough to eat a damn cookie. Imagine that. You know what?

I'm curious to see where all this nonsense is leading to, or even whether it is going to end somewhere because, the way things are going, this may end like those crazy movies with an "open ending." Boy, I hate that. But remember, Annie Joseph, if you don't empower yourself to be here, you'll simply lose your job. Does this mean my boss is controlling my life? Wait, I'm confused. Seminars like this make people go nuts. When she was telling the Lisa story, I started wondering whether I'd chosen the right career. How stupid is that?

"OK, so this is our first assignment – if you want to call it that. We are going to use the power of "permission." For the next month, I want you to pay attention when you empower yourself. I want you to watch whether you're really the one holding that power or whether you've willingly placed the power in someone else's hand. Watch and see whether you allow yourself to have a pleasant life, pleasant thoughts and pleasant people around you. Sit and watch. I also want you to think whether you empower yourself to keep coming to these meetings or not, and whether you've really put these teachings into practice. Don't forget that for us to have an opinion about something, we need to be familiar with it. And for those who plan to continue to come, put these teachings into practice through something that you truly enjoy doing. If you enjoy painting, express what you've learned by painting a picture. If you play an instrument, use music as a means of expression. If you like to write, start a journal. I won't tell you how to do it. That's for you to decide. All I ask you to do is to tell us how you expressed what you learned today.

"Good night, everyone. I hope you'll empower yourselves to be back here in body and soul so we can continue to learn what Cinderella has to teach us."

What Cinderella has to teach us? I still don't have a clue. What I do know is I'm going to get the hell out of here, scarf down those almond cookies and watch the shows I recorded with TiVo. I still haven't found my diet sheet. Maybe it's a sign that the diet sucks. All right, I'll start Monday.

At least I should get a good story out of this. What a bunch of con artists. I can read the headline now: "Stuck in Cinder-hell-a."

And now I can go home. Go home where I have no one to share all this with. Ah-ha, Annie, stop complaining: You were the one who decided to stop getting involved after the disappointment with your ex. I wonder whether I can empower myself to stay single? I'm already beginning to sound like Cathy. This group is starting to mess with my head. I'd better get something to eat because my real problem is obviously hunger.

Chapter 3

RSW (Really Stupid Woman)

It's been a week since I attended my first session of "Cinder-hell-a." Obviously, I haven't embraced the idea. I seem incapable of putting any of it into practice. At work it's still the same old, same old. Every day I feel more like eating, or digging into that file of dessert recipes that I keep for my food stories. Even if I don't try them out, I like to read them: Chocolate-Mint Cookies, Maple-Walnut Espresso Torte, Glazed Hazelnut Mousse Cake ... Mmmm. It's like Porn for Fatties.

For the last seven days, I haven't stopped rehearsing how to tell Paige to assign someone else to this project. I have no desire to go to the meetings. You know those moments in life when words like "new life," "success" and "happiness" make sense only in self-help books? That's where I am. I've also convinced myself that I will royally screw up this story and the fairy-tale fascists will slap Women & Co. with a libel suit. So, instead of doing research for the project, I'm fixating on food. I want to throw my nightly Lean Cuisine in the trash and get up the guts to go to the Italian restaurant just around the corner from my house. I like to go there in spite of the "poor-thing-it-must-be-horrible-to-eat-by-yourself-in-public" looks.

"Good morning, Annie. I need to see you in my office."

Wow. The Big Boss actually came to my cubicle to fetch me? That's a first. I didn't think she even knew where I sat.

"Sure, Paige."

Best be pleasant right from the start, especially if I have to tell her I want to drop out of the project. Now is the time to be strong. Speak up, Annie!

"Annie, I wanted to tell you how thrilled I am that you accepted this job. Your article could be a cover story. We know a lot of celebrities belong to this group, and I think some of them might even be willing to give us an interview. You've been with us for five years now. This new responsibility will be good for you. You deserve this opportunity, and I'm sure I won't regret having picked you for this assignment. How was the first meeting?"

After all this, how can I ask her to replace me?

"It was, it was … great. Interesting. It was just the beginning. There isn't much to say yet, so it'll be a while before I start the writing process."

"I understand you're supposed to practice their teachings. Have you started on that?"

"No, I mean, l almost …"

"Don't forget: It's really important that you get into it right away and practice their teachings as best as you can. Do you remember Gabrielle's story 'Doing Time at the Country's Trendiest Spa'? Well, she followed everything to a 'T.' She lost weight, and not only did she end up on the cover of the magazine but she also met her husband."

That's just terrific. Then why doesn't she assign me to do a "Life in a Five-Star Resort" story? Instead, I'm writing about "Life in a Crazy Fairy-Tale Cult." There's no way I'll have the same results as Gabrielle – as if she ever needed to lose weight. Why? So she can fit in a size double-zero instead of a zero? Wait a minute, let's rewind a minute here: Did she say Gabrielle is getting married? So she's not dating Ben? Nah, a guy like that could NOT be single.

"I can't wait to read the whole article. Was there anything you wanted to talk about?"

Yes, I did. I wanted to say that I'm going to quit this assignment, but as a really spineless woman – a coward who can't say what she feels or thinks – I'm going to slink back to my office and put these moronic teachings into practice. From now on, I'll check how I empower myself to keep my thoughts and feelings to myself. I always empower myself to keep quiet when I really want to say something. I'm sick of it.

"No, not at all. Thanks for this opportunity, Paige. I'll keep your tip in mind and get down to it body and soul. The article will be great."

Now there's really no way out. So I'm going to sit in front of the computer and empower myself to write about what I learned from the first meeting. Hmmm, what gives me pleasure? Does anything, really? This is awful. I don't even know what I find pleasurable. Well, when I was in college – no, wait, since I was a child, I really did love to write. I always kept a diary. I just loved writing long, newsy letters, filled with funny stories and detailed descriptions, to my parents and friends on their birthdays. I was young and foolish back then – before writing became something you did to pay the rent. I used to dream about publishing a book.

That's when I started writing short stories. I bound them together and everything. But I never had the courage to publish them. That "book" is in a box in my closet's darkest corner. When I feel too tired and deflated to write new stories, I still sometimes dig out that first volume and read the stories. You know what? They comfort me. Yes, I actually do love writing. My dream is to become a "real" writer – the type of scribe who is both popular and critically acclaimed and gets rigorous endorsements from Oprah's book club. I'm going to express my perception of the Cinderella meetings through words. Come on, sister, let's get the ball rolling. Let's write!

So, what did I get from that meeting? Come on, Annie Joseph. Be brave. You were born healthy. Empower yourself to do this assignment; it can be the biggest opportunity of your life. Oh, man, am I actually resisting doing this because I don't empower myself to accept new opportunities? But Paige picked me because I'm a nobody, remember? Still, she did choose me, so now the opportunity and the power are in my hands. What the hell do I empower myself to do in this life, dammit? I empower myself to work hard, and to be cranky, lonely and loveless. I empower myself to reject the possibility that my life can change. I empower myself to reject the fact that I can find someone and be happy. I empower myself to refuse to believe in my talents. Am I capable of anything? I empower myself to not feel pleasure. I empower myself to be undervalued by others. That's enough. Now I know what to write.

AS OF TODAY, I EMPOWER MYSELF …

… TO FEEL APPRECIATED, EVEN WHEN OTHERS DON´T ACKNOWLEDGE MY VALUE.

… TO GIVE LOVE A SECOND CHANCE, EVEN IF MY HEART WANTS TO KEEP ITS DOORS SHUT.

… TO FEEL PLEASURE, EVEN IF GUILT AND FEAR TRY TO TAKE IT AWAY FROM ME.

… TO TRUST MY TALENTS, EVEN IF I'VE GOTTEN USED TO BELITTLING THEM.

… TO OVERCOME MY LIMITATIONS, EVEN IF I'VE STOPPED FACING THEM.

… TO BELIEVE IN HAPPY ENDINGS, EVEN WHEN I ALWAYS THOUGHT THEY WERE UNACHIEVABLE.

What is this I've written? I sound like a self-help junkie. Ahhh, all it needs is a signature. I tap out three letters on the keyboard. RSW.

Really Stupid Woman! That's how I feel when I practice anything from that seminar. But it beats being unemployed. My little testament may be stupid, but at least I don't have to show it to anyone. I push Control-S to save it, then name the file "RSW." It's a start, anyway. I'll keep it for a few days and maybe it will give me something to build a bigger story on. Ooh, I really need to pee.

As I head out the door, I realize I've forgotten to send my latest recipe to the editors. But I've really gotta go. Besides, what is Ashley good for if not to occasionally help me out? I spot her standing outside Jane's cubicle – gossiping, as usual. I call her name.

"Could you do me a huge favor? I need to send that 'Raspberry Salad with Walnuts' recipe to Paige as soon as possible. Could you do it for me? It's on my computer."

Before she can respond, I'm already charging down the hall toward the rest room.

Well, that took forever. Why is there always a line in the women's rest room? Even at work. That's a mystery that needs to be solved. And once I got through that line I had to stop by the vending machine for another Diet Coke. It's the only way I can stay awake in the afternoon. What? This can't be happening! Paige is actually standing by my cubicle, with a look like she wants to talk to me. Maybe Ashley forgot to send her the recipe and she wants to know where it is. But it seems unlikely she'd make a personal appearance to track down a silly recipe. I have to be imagining this.

"Oh, Annie, there you are. I just got this first-person piece from you about empowering yourself."

I can't believe what she's saying. How on earth did she get my RSW piece?

Somebody up there in heaven, please help me! Angels, elves, fairies, my dear mother – if you save me from this one, I swear I'll adopt a small child from Bangladesh. I'll go to church every Sunday. I'll pray the rosary every day. If Paige finds out I wrote this flaky, New Age-y list, I'll end up writing a story called "How To Lose Your Job in Five Minutes."

"Oh, um ... that RSW piece? Isn't it silly? A friend of mine wrote it. It must have been sent to you by mistake. You know how it is, I mean, she's by herself in a new city. Loneliness can do that to you. Anyway, I was going to throw it out."

"I'm glad you didn't do that. I really loved it."

"Uhhh, didn't you think the article was a little simplistic?"

I can feel my face flushing red. I stammer on.

"There's nothing really special about it."

"I disagree completely! It's precisely that simplicity that will touch people's hearts. There is no fancy pop psychology here, no jargon. She cuts straight to the point with this simple, accessible wisdom. What is your friend's name anyway? What does RSW stand for?"

"Oh, yes, um, that's her nickname. I don't know her real name. We're Internet friends. I don't know her personally. And I have no idea what those initials mean. I never really asked her. I'm afraid she may say something weird. She's really strange."

"She may be a little strange, but she sounds delightful. Can you ask her whether she'd be interested in publishing this in our next issue? Our readers would love it. This is the type of inspirational thing they need."

"Uh, I don't know whether that'll be possible. It's kind of like a private thing. See, she writes all those things just for me."

"So give me her phone number, and I'll have someone call her."

Oh, my God, I just keep digging myself deeper and deeper.

"I don't have her phone number. She's really bizarre; she suffers from ... some social phobias. But I'll e-mail her and ask whether she'd be interested."

"Perceptive people like your friend are so in touch with their inner world. If you're too busy working on the fairy tale story, I can have my assistant e-mail her and explain how it all works so she doesn't get scared or intimidated by the whole thing."

"You don't have to do that, Paige. I can take care of it, no problem. RSW asked me not to give her e-mail address to anyone."

"My intuition never fails me. This is the type of article our readers would love. I'll be looking forward to her reply."

Why? Why do these things happen to me? And why did Ashley send that piece to her? I'd always thought she was basically harmless, if irritating. Now I have to wonder whether she wanted me to look foolish in front of Paige. Maybe she wants my job.

And now I'm going to have to let pushy Paige publish my confessions. Wait a minute. They're not my confessions. As far as she knows, they're RSW's confessions. But Paige will probably send a SWAT team across the country to find RSW. And how will they pay someone who doesn't exist? She doesn't even have a Social Security number. On the other hand, Paige has more determination than a pit bull. Even if I say RSW doesn't want it published, she'll continue to hammer at me about letting her contact my friend – my crazy, anonymous, agoraphobic, Kumbaya-singing, imaginary friend. What a mess. Well, I'll figure it out later. I'll let them publish it. Maybe our readers will all laugh at it and that will be the end of it. In fact, I'm positive they will. Who wouldn't?

Where is that damned Ashley when you need to talk to her anyway? Wait, here she comes. I'd better get to the bottom of this.

"Ashley, why did you send that piece to Paige?"

I'm struggling to stay composed. She looks a little hurt.

"I thought you told me to. You said Paige needed that recipe."

"The recipe!"

My voice is wavering with fury.

"I wanted you to send the 'Raspberry Salad with Walnuts' recipe. It is labeled that, as plain as can be."

"But the document said RSW! I thought you were abbreviating 'Raspberry Salad with Walnuts.' Oh, never mind."

Ashley is in full defensive mode. I snap, striding out of our cubicle. What are the odds my random abbreviation could actually be confused with a salad recipe? Still, I can understand her confusion. It was an honest mistake. I probably should apologize. But first I need to speak to Paige.

I stick my head into Paige's office.

"Hey, Paige. I got RSW's reply already. I can't believe how quickly she replied; she must never leave her computer. Anyway, she authorized the publication."

This is fabulous. I've been to only one of the damn meetings and things are already getting out of hand. How is this all going to end?

Chapter 4

Cinderella in a Very Tight Spot!

It *is again D-Day – what I like to think of as that Damned Fairy Tale Thing. Just moments before "class" begins, I flop into the folding chair beside my new "Cinder-buddy" Liz. I sigh heavily as I think of the wasted two hours before me – two hours that could be spent doing something much more stimulating. Like color-coding my sock drawer. Liz's cheery voice interrupts my self-pitying reverie.*

"Welcome to our second meeting!"

It seems like real enthusiasm.

"I'm so happy to see you here. I hope you had a productive and enriching four weeks of practice."

Oh, honey, it was enriching all right! Now I have double personality disorder: I'm a frustrated journalist by day and a sociophobic writer by night. Liz is completely oblivious to my scowl.

"Oh, Annie, I'd like to give you a little something after the meeting. It's a few slices of apple pie that I baked for you. I thought you'd like it. I know how you young career women never have time to bake, and apple pie just happens to be my specialty."

"Wow! Thank you very much, Liz."

What a nice person, this Liz. Gosh, it's been so long since anybody gave me anything that it feels a little strange – even if it's just apple pie. Fine, from now on, I'll allow myself to receive good things from people. Good things? Well, first let's see how the meeting turns out today.

Cathy comes in and says nothing, turning her back on us and scrawling "Cinderella: The Real Story," on a white board in large, loopy letters. She turns to the class and wastes no time getting to the point.

"Good evening, everyone. Glad to see you all here. Now we've got lots to cover tonight, so I'm going to dive right into the lesson. We are going to briefly review that tale you've heard a thousand times – 'Cinderella' – so we can later apply it to our second teaching. I could use several other versions, but I prefer to stick to the version my mother used to tell me as a child:

" 'Once upon a time there was a kind widower who married a very arrogant and cold-hearted widow who, unfortunately, had two daughters exactly like her.

" 'The widower was the father of a very kind, young, cheerful and generous girl, with a heart full of love. Her name was Cinderella.

" 'After her dear father's untimely death, Cinderella was forced to work day and night, cleaning the house and doing other heavy household chores. In spite of doing her absolute best, Cinderella received only scorn and humiliation both from her stepmother and her stepdaughters. Her only friends were the little animals in the house. But Cinderella always had the hope in her heart that one day her life would change.' "

Dear God, please don't let anyone find out I belong to the "Fairy Club," where outwardly normal-looking adults spend their Thursday evenings recapturing the "magic" of Cinderella's life story.

" 'One day the King had a ball at the palace with the women in his kingdom as his guests. From among them, his son was to choose a young lady to marry. There was general excitement. Cinderella wanted to go very much. Her stepmother agreed, but only if she finished all her chores and somehow found a way to furnish her own pretty gown for the ball.

" 'Cinderella was determined to go. So she finished all her work, helped her stepsisters get dressed, cut up some of her stepsisters' gowns and transformed the pieces into her own beautiful dress.

" 'When the two sisters saw Cinderella, they recognized the fabrics on their stepsister's gown so they tore it up. They left for the ball laughing. Cinderella was so sad she began to cry inconsolably. She was starting to lose hope.

" 'Then all of a sudden, her fairy godmother appeared with her magic wand in hand. She turned Cinderella's ragged clothes into a gorgeous gown and her shabby shoes into exquisite crystal slippers. Then she touched a pumpkin with her magic wand and transformed it into a beautiful carriage.

Finally she tapped the little house pets with her magic wand, turning them into two coachmen and four beautiful horses. Cinderella was so happy she started jumping up and down with pure joy. The fairy godmother warned her that all this magical transformation would last only until midnight.

" 'As soon as Cinderella entered the palace, all eyes were on the beautiful and mysterious young woman. The prince had eyes only for her and he danced with her all night long. Cinderella almost missed her midnight magic curfew and had to leave in a rush, inadvertently losing her crystal slipper on the staircase. She didn't even try to pick it up because she knew there was no time.' "

I really can't wait to hear what kind of "Very Important Moral" Cathy now plans to teach us. It will probably be something insightful such as: "Dumping your boyfriend in a rush will cause you to lose the Manolo Blahniks you bought on sale last year."

" 'The prince was madly in love with Cinderella and swore he would do whatever he could to find her. So he knocked on every door in the kingdom, asking all the young women to try on the slipper. Finally, he knocked on Cinderella's door.

" 'The mean sisters were eager to try on the shoe, but their feet were way too big and clumsy and they couldn't jam them in the tiny crystal slipper, no matter how many times they tried.

" 'When Cinderella wanted to try it on, her stepsisters made fun of her and laughed out loud. The laughter stopped short as soon as they saw how well Cinderella's foot fit into the tiny slipper.

" 'At that very moment, her fairy godmother appeared and once again turned Cinderella's ragged clothes into a beautiful gown. The wicked stepmother and her daughters fell on their knees and asked the *queen* of the ball for forgiveness. Cinderella gave them a big hug and forgave them with all her heart. She married the prince and they lived happily ever after.' "

Happily ever after? Who still buys this crap besides those single, lonely and desperate women who insist on living happily ever after in a society in which we are tired of seeing a lot of "I do" transforming into "I do want to kill you." Cathy speaks again.

"By looking around the room, I can tell some of you are wondering: How can this fairy tale make my life better? The Greek philosopher Epictetus said that men are distressed not by things but by the opinions they draw from them. As I said in our first meeting, the elements of this story are symbols that represent our internal world and the way we cope with our external world. In Cinderella's story the union between the prince and the princess symbolizes this. I hope these teachings help you find your deepest strengths and discover absolute fulfillment."

Aah, my favorite adenoidal friend has returned for a second round. Steve turns to his "audience" and chuckles sarcastically.

"Yeah, who knows, perhaps soon we will too find our fairy godmother and fulfill all the desires of our heart."

"You're absolutely right, Steve. I hope each one of you can find his or her "fairy godmother" while practicing these teachings. In spite of this fairy tale's lighthearted tone, it is important to bring this point to the surface."

And the Pope is canonizing Cathy as we speak, for she can officially be deemed a saint for putting up with Steve, my adorable but pesky soul mate in the cheap sweater. Cathy continues to blather on about fairies and destiny, reminding me of "Women and Mythology," a course I took at Columbia.

"Many stories are characterized by the presence of the fairy factor. The word *fairy* comes from the Latin *fata*, which means *god of destiny*. The most important thing in all this is to find our destiny by following the right path. Cinderella didn't accomplish this in a magical New York second. She went through a lot of hardship and suffering before she found her destiny. This is a true trait of heroes: overcoming trials while finding their destiny – the true meaning of their existence."

I struggle hard to shift my concentration back to Cathy, so perfectly groomed in a chocolate suit and swirled paisley scarf. Destiny? Here we go! Now watch her unroll the secret scrolls of Humanity's Destiny.

"So, what you're saying is we all have a destiny – something pre-determined?"

"Beatrice, let's just say we have a path to follow, a mission to accomplish. Do you know how many people feel empty and dissatisfied with their lives? So many of us are programmed to believe the answer to happiness is making money. But how many times have we seen people with tons of money who spend their lives looking for satisfaction? How can we fill this emptiness? Certainly not with our bank accounts. So, what is it that we're so anxious to find but have a hard time finding? Destiny is the act of discovering the path that our soul wants so desperately to find."

Steve isn't about to let her get by that easily.

"Isn't this 'soul business' just a little too mystical for a bunch of modern, well-educated people to believe?"

He glances back at the crowd, as if for reassurance. I smile at him, even as I'm thinking how unusually quizzical he is. Maybe he's writing a story, too? Judging by the acrylic sweater and I-live-in-my-mom's-basement skin tone, it's for some techno-geek magazine.

"The idea that every human being has a destiny or a mission in life does not originate from fortune-tellers or visionaries. The Greek philosopher Plato expressed this idea in *The Republic*. He said that before birth all of us receive a *daimon*, a soul companion who guides us in fulfilling our destiny."

"So what you're saying is all we have to do sit around waiting for a guy named Fate to knock on our door with the crystal slipper we lost at last month's party?"

"Well, Steve, Cinderella actually didn't wait for destiny to knock on her door. Let's say she was able to open the door and let her destiny enter. But how can we open the door of a fulfilled destiny and live happily ever after? How can we attract the power of a "fairy godmother" to create a miracle in our hardest moments? Everybody wants to be happy. Everybody wants a better destiny. Why is it hard to achieve?"

"Because the fairy godmother has some favorites, and I am sure I am not one of them."

Steve, I am on your team, buddy!

"Steve, you're focusing on the wrong issue. It is not about your fairy godmother. The power is all within you. As it was with Cinderella. You control your own magic wand. It is easy to believe that with the wave of a magic wand all of our problems will disappear, but that is not reality and it is truly not how Cinderella made her life better. In our meetings we are going to have the opportunity to see what she did in order to attract the miracle in her life, and I wish that each of you can at least try to apply this to your life and see the results, even if you don't believe it, even if it seems too "fairy tale." I want to challenge each of you to see another view of this story and prove that I am wrong. The only way that you can truly prove that I am wrong is to practice it."

Good old Mr. Reliable Steve. At least he makes the meetings more interesting. Still, I'd better keep an eye on him. It would be just my luck to finally get a big assignment and then be scooped by Dungeons & Dragons magazine's star reporter.

"Let's say that the "fairy godmother," "her destiny," "her miracle" was always there. It's like an apple seed that has all the potential to become an apple even when you can't see it. In order to have apples, you have to plant the seed in good soil, take care and wait, and one day, "like a miracle," you look outside and see a beautiful tree with a lot of apples.

"So, in order to attract the fairy godmother, in order to prepare the land to create miracles in her life, Cinderella did something ..."

"What did she do?"

Oops! I couldn't resist.

"She did what I want you to practice these next weeks. I want you to: GIVE YOUR BEST EVEN WHEN YOU DON'T WANT TO."

To emphasize it she writes it on the whiteboard in big, black letters.

"And that's one of the things that Cinderella did to create miracles in her life: She gave her best. In her hardest moments, instead of complaining she chose to work hard and treat others with kindness and generosity. Think about the areas of your life in which you can be better, in which you can react in a better way. Famed psychologist Abraham Maslow said man has a natural tendency to want to become a more complete human being. This is our nature; this is who we are. We are made to become the best that we can be. And if you want to fulfill your destiny, if you want 'the help of the fairy godmother,' you have to respect your natural tendency to be a better person, to become a more complete human being. Believe me, there are a lot of moments in our lives in which we choose not to give our best. So this week empower yourself to do your best. Instead of giving anger, give compassion. Instead of disillusion, give hope. Instead of complaining, give solutions."

And where could I exercise this Mother Teresa of Calcutta act? With Ashley, the most annoying intern in a three-county area? With Gabrielle, the magazine's most conceited writer? With Ben, who will forever remember me as "Jovial Annie," the idiot who spilled coffee on him? Whoops, shouldn't have let my mind wander into that territory. As pathetic as it seems, I'd been daydreaming about him ever since our first meeting – if you could call it that. Even in that short time, he'd seemed like such a nice guy – not at all like the stuck-up jerk I'd imagined him to be. And he'd been so kind about the whole coffee thing, even though I made a total ass out of myself. Cathy's voice, unfortunately, interrupts my thoughts.

"Do you usually give your best? Do you practice kindness and generosity?"

Her eyes scan the crowd, as they do whenever she asks one of her many rhetorical questions.

"Hi, Cathy. My name is Louise. I'm not going to lie to you. The reason I joined this group is because it helped my sister change her life, mainly financially. I also want to prosper. Is this second practice going to help me financially? I mean, my personal experience with rich people is they're not very kind and most of them are just not that generous. It looks like being kind doesn't fit very well in our competitive, materialistic world."

Steve, Louise and I, the back-seat becklers. But I totally agree with Louise. If Cinderella were living in the 21st century, she would have given her stepmom a few whacks on the head and put out a contract on the stepsisters. At the internationally televised "Cinderella trials," her publicity-seeking celebrity attorneys would have appeared with their notorious client on "Oprah," where they blamed it all on child abuse, or depression, or dishpan hands. Case dismissed. How can Cathy sell this?

"We must watch how we interpret our external world. You obviously are one of the many people who measure other people's prosperity by the size of their bank accounts. But I can guarantee that your sister's financial success was actually the result of healthy attitudes that made her prosperous, not only financially but also in all areas of life. People who make money dishonestly are satisfied with very little."

"Very little?"

Louise doesn't look too happy. Poor thing. She probably thought she was signing up for Donald Trump's Become-a-Millionaire-in-a-Weekend Seminar, and now she has to listen to fairy tales.

"Of course. These people will do anything and everything to obtain money and fame, but never have real prosperity – a word that means enrichment and growth. We want you to grow in all areas: personal, professional, romantic, financial. Why limit yourself to just one area when you deserve it all?"

"And to practice goodness will help me acquire all this?"

"That is the big question. We live in a time in which we are taught to pursue – to conquer the world. Our group proposes that you pursue your forgotten internal world – that you cultivate hidden strengths. In the process, you don't *do* everything, but *be* everything to draw the world to yourselves. There's the difference. As the Chinese proverb says, if you want to get a year of prosperity, plant grains; if you want to get ten years of prosperity, plant trees; but if you want to get one hundred years of prosperity, develop people."

"I'm slightly confused."

And so am I, Louise. Confused and eager to eat the apple pie Liz brought me. I think it's so great for a woman her age to believe her life can still change for the better. Sometimes I actually feel like helping her find her daughter. It wouldn't cost me anything. All I have to do is ask Ashley to play Sherlock Holmes. That girl just loves to play detective.

"Let's be practical: How many stories do we know of people who work, work, work and feel they're getting nowhere?"

Cathy, honey, that's just the story of my life. I run all day and worry like crazy. I'm like a hamster in a wheel.

"And how do these people face adverse situations? Do they complain? Or do they compare their life with that of others? It's no good to just work – to just do things while forgetting to be a better human being. If you want to get the best from life, you must give your best. The Bible story of Joseph is an example of someone whose kindness helped him reach his destiny. Like Cinderella, Joseph was humiliated by his brothers and ended up being sold as a slave to a caravan heading for Egypt. In spite of all the opposing circumstances he experienced, Joseph persevered and retained his essential goodness. So, in the next four weeks, we're going to practice empowering ourselves by giving our best, by exercising traits such as kindness, love and joy. We'll start with ourselves. Do you give the best to yourself? Do you allow yourself to have pleasant moments? Do you empower yourself by eating healthy or by eating junk food?"

OK, lady – yeah, kindness has a lot to do with my diet. Anytime I snap at Ashley or almost lose it with a snippy saleslady who suggests I try the "plus section," it's because I've eaten junk food. I can see I'm not the only one who finds Cathy's words ludicrous; Steve shoots out of his chair as if it's on fire.

"What do you mean offering our best? And what has the body got to do with it?"

"Steve, to act in the best possible way is to try to make choices that create a positive outcome. And we can understand this idea only if we become generous, by putting ourselves in someone else's shoes and giving our absolute best to that person. The main reason some people can't lose weight successfully is their lack of generosity."

Not only am I a fat pig, but I also happen to be a fat, stingy pig, according to this nut job. Damn, I've even lost my appetite. Now I have to say something.

"I don't understand, Cathy. I don't see how the Cinderella story really carries all these themes – generosity, destiny, obesity."

"Good point, Annie."

And don't think you're going to get on my good side just because you remembered my name. I want a straightforward answer for once, and I won't settle for your habit of answering questions with other questions.

"When I say that characteristics such as kindness and generosity help us fulfill our mission, I cannot leave them out of the relationship we develop with ourselves. You have to be generous with yourself first. I would be promoting the inequality that is prevalent in the world today. When I say generosity helps you build your body and lose weight, I'm not making things more complicated. I'm actually making them easier. The moment we realize our body is a crucial instrument in helping us to fulfill our mission, we can't neglect it anymore. You're not what you eat. You eat what you are!"

Well that may look great on a bumper sticker, but that doesn't mean it makes sense. I'm not about to back down.

"Quite frankly, I still don't get it."

Pretty soon, Cathy is going to dole out brochures on some miracle weight-loss supplements. Aha! So this is actually some underground group for frustrated fatties.

"If you are a generous person – someone who is generous to yourself – you will choose food that's good for your body and overcome overeating – not only to fit into your favorite dress or to look good for a reunion. You'll do it for love: love for your body, the instrument that allows you to work toward your fulfillment."

I subtly scan the crowd, and am greeted by looks of bewilderment and skepticism. Still, I have to admit nobody looks bored. A short, plumpish brunette stands.

"Hi, my name is Kate and I have a question: Does choosing good food help us change our life? I feel like I'm stuck. I never seem to find that special someone in my life. I'm like a gutter: I seem to collect only trash."

Gutsy lady! I would never confess out loud that I feel stuck. And not just stuck, trapped! Cathy flashes that familiar smile – as if she's explaining the most basic of multiplication tables to second-graders.

"Kate, a hero's greatness is exercised in small ways. If you're unable to say no to some food that's detrimental to your health, what makes you think you'll be capable of saying 'no' to the other junk in your life – unhealthy relationships? We offer our best after we recognize our greatness, the hero in us. The moment we're beaten by a glass of alcohol, by a drag on a cigarette or even by a strong impulse, that's the moment we forget our greatness and stop being heroes. The buildup of small attitudes is what's going to incite a major transformation in our lives. Lao Tse said, 'He who is victorious over others is strong; however, he who's victorious over himself is omnipotent.' "

I see her point.

"In the next few weeks, we're going to practice Cinderella's heroic virtues. When we offer our best to the world, the world gives us its best in return. So, for the next few weeks, concentrate on always giving your best. Do it for yourselves and for others. Before you leave your house, ask yourselves: Is this the best outfit I can wear? Is this the best smile I can offer? Is this the best way to treat people? Is this the best food for my body? Is this the best answer I can give? So, I hope all of you will try out these practices and have a fantastic week! Oh, and before I forget: It might not be easy to apply these practices to your life. These thoughts and actions are unfamiliar to you and will take much practice before they feel normal. When you come across hardship, always remember that if you continue acting the way you've always acted, you'll continue living as you've always lived. Have a great week!"

A great week? After all the information I just received, I predict I'll have the worst week in history. My mind is so busy sifting and sorting through Cathy's words that I drive home by rote. "Will the next days be a little easier?" I keep asking myself aloud. I find myself so relieved to be back in the warm cocoon of my apartment. It's not much, but it's all mine – from the excellent knock-off of a Persian rug in front of my IKEA couch. On the bookcase shelves I display my most treasured possessions: my favorite books, the pottery I've picked up at flea markets, and the fancy china tea cups I inherited from Nana.

I kick off my sensible clogs, pad across the hardwood floors and, by habit, flick on the TV. The sound of television news fills the room as I check the soil of "Phil," the faithful philodendron that I've owned for six years. Looks like Phil is thirsty again. Hah! They say if you can keep a plant alive, you're ready to keep a relationship alive. Interesting that they chose to equate plants with men. Maybe that's because when you ask either one a question, you'll get a similar response.

Into the kitchen to get Phil a drink, and then station myself in front of the refrigerator. What can I eat to make myself feel better? Should I scarf down those tempting slices of pie, prepared especially for me by Liz, or should I microwave that last chicken with broccoli Lean Cuisine in the freezer? Instead of dinner, I usually reach for anything that tastes slightly sweet. I know, I know. It's not the healthiest habit, but the sugar somehow helps all the pain and the frustration of the day disappear. Who cares if I feel fat and hopeless afterward? What matters is that I get immediate relief.

And don't think I haven't tried to change my "sweet" habit. If I had $5 for every diet I've started, I could afford to pay a top plastic surgeon to suck all the fat away. There's always some major "force of nature" – I'm premenstrual, it's the holidays, I'm depressed and need a lift – that prevents me from sticking to a diet. Problem is, I need to practice these teachings or this story won't work and I'll probably lose my job.

Ah, Cathy, why did you have to say all that? After hearing your words of "wisdom," I've realized I've become the biggest glutton on the face of the earth. Whenever Mom made me, as a child, wear dresses that made me look like the Pillsbury Doughboy, I channeled all my anger on my doll Mindy by calling her a pig and pulling off her head. Now I've transferred the abuse to myself – minus, ahem, the beheading. But I can't do it anymore. I feel like a selfish fat pig whose mantra is "me, me and more me"! I think only about my own satisfaction with complete disregard to the damage I do to my body and soul.

On the other hand, it's easy for Cathy to say all this. She's Miss I Wear a Size 8 and Have Never Had To Diet in My Life. She obviously doesn't know what it's like to have food as your only friend. Just realizing how dependent I am on it is making my mood sink even lower. Maybe I can snap out of it by loading up on the all-you-can-eat buffet. Just try to stop me, Little Miss Perfect Cathy. Bring it on, sister! You're lucky you never had to cope by overloading your pancreas with heaps of sugar! Hah! Wow! Hold on for a second. Now that I put it that way, I never really thought of it this way. I'm all hung up on the taste and the immediate pleasure with total disregard for the damage I'm doing to my body. My poor body – struggling to keep everything on an even keel – even when I feed it nothing but fat and preservatives and sugar. All right, Miss Cinderella, you win this round – chicken and broccoli, it is.

After eating a halfway-decent meal, I actually feel good. I'm going shopping tomorrow – to the organic food section. Oh, sweet victory! This is the problem with having household appliances for roommates: You wind up talking to yourself and have no one to share your small victories with. God, I miss Mom, but I'm not going to focus on that. Instead, I'm going to pick out my best outfit for tomorrow and go to work with a big smile on my face. I bet my co-workers won't miss my black baggy dress. They probably think it's been painted on my body. Let's see, oh my gawd! My closet looks like the rack at the Funeral Home Thrift Store. OK, here's the best outfit I have: a simple knit dress in a really flattering deep shade of purple. I think I've even got a silk scarf to match it somewhere. It's going to feel so weird to go to work all dressed up, but I have to look at this from a practical standpoint: I have to put Cathy's words into practice so I can write about it and keep my job.

Chapter 5

Like a Hollywood Movie

"**Wow,** you look amazing today! I didn't recognize you for a minute."

Do I even have to tell you this came out of Ashley's mouth?

"What's going on? Are you in love or something?"

I have a little request for you Ashley: SHUT UP! Wait, maybe that's not the best answer. Remember Annie, if you want to get the best out of life, you've got to offer your best – even to a nuisance like Ashley. I turn and give her my sweetest smile.

"Oh, honey, I am in love – with life. Have a great day, Ashley."

Oh my gawd! Who am I? A walking incarnation of "Chicken Soup for the Soul"? And all before 9 a.m. I must be possessed – by Cinderella! Maybe Cathy secretly hypnotized us last night. Still, a little milk of human kindness is worth it, just to see the stunned look on Ashley's face.

"Annie, I can't get over this. You look so different. Oh, wait, before I forget. Your dad called yesterday. That face tells me you're not going to call him back, right?"

"Right."

"He sounds like such a sweet old man. What on earth has he done to deserve such a cold shoulder?"

Ashley, if you continue to bother me, I may be forced to gently shove a crystal slipper down your throat! OK, let's practice holding the temper and count crystal slippers instead – nice, tranquil crystal slippers, filled with peace, serenity and love for thy neighbor: 100, 107, 17,002.

"I'm sorry, but I'd rather not talk about this right now. It's a weird family thing. All families are dysfunctional to some extent, and mine is no different."

Thanks to Cinderella, I'm turning into a polite idiot – a polite, overdressed idiot. But I guess it beats the heck out of being the same, bitter Annie Joseph. Ashley regains her composure.

"Of course, my family also has its share of problems. You should see my brother – what a head case. If you ever need someone to talk to ..."

And ABC presents the hottest new nighttime soap: "Desperate Cubicle Mates." Just then, Ashley slaps her hand against her forehead – a gesture she performs with great drama whenever she believes she has just recalled something of great importance.

"Oh, I have another message I completely forgot to tell you! Paige wants to speak with you ASAP. Sorry I didn't mention something sooner. I was so taken back when I saw you all dressed up, with that pretty dress, lipstick, even high heels! Don't think I've ever seen you look so nice. Usually my memory's so good. I must be in shock."

Ah, only Ashley can make me feel like it's some sort of freakish aberration if I don't show up at the office in a garbage bag. And in the process, she nearly gets me in trouble with Paige. I head to her office immediately.

My newly acquired Cinderella mentality has definitely saved Ashley's life. What does Paige want now? Let me guess, she probably thought I looked like a clown in these clothes so she's going to invite me to brighten up her son's birthday party. No wait, she wanted to see me before she saw the "new" me. I have to admit I've spoken to her more in the last two weeks than I did in the previous five years. God, I hope they didn't figure out who I was at the Association of Eternally Frustrated Joy-Seekers. I pop my head into Paige's office.

"Good morning, Paige. I heard you were looking for me?"

"Yes, yes, please sit down. Wow, Annie, I must say you look so … different! That color really enhances your hair and skin. You look five years younger!"

"Oh, um, thank you, Paige."

All right, I confess: I love compliments. But, who doesn't?

"I called you because I want to talk to you about RSW."

Ouch! I bet she knows I'm RSW. I've been so busy worrying about Cinderella-ville that I'd forgotten about that stupid piece. I'll bet the article was a total disaster. Oh my gawd! I'm so getting fired! Now I'm a terrible reporter and a liar! I struggle to look calm.

"RSW? What's wrong with her?"

"Well, we published her article in this month's issue. It's been on the stand for three days and ..."

I find myself blurting out excuses.

"Well, Paige, I did mention that this article was unusual and that RSW was kind of unusual."

"Our readers didn't seem to think so."

Great! The article unleashed a suicide wave around the country.

"Um, really? What did they say?"

Paige leans back in her leather chair, smiles and elegantly touches her folded-up designer eyewear to her chin, as if she were posing for a Vanity Fair cover story.

"They absolutely loved it. Some readers actually said they read the article out loud and felt something special, and their day instantly became better. We've never received so many e-mails in such a short period of time, not even when Gabrielle did her piece on plastic surgery horror stories. Many of them are asking us to publish another article by RSW, preferably on our Web site so they could read it before the magazine hits the stands."

I can't believe this. I used to spend weeks laboring over food stories and didn't hear a peep. But I spend a few minutes writing something for my journal, and it turns into Women & Co.'s greatest hit. Suddenly, I feel like wiping off all the eye makeup I applied so carefully this mornin. I really do feel like a clown now.

"I don't understand all of this response for such simple words. I don't even see it as a real article. For me it looks more like a draft of a fake poem."

"Annie, sometimes we don't need a lot of words to express profound thoughts. I read the article myself this morning. And you know what? It's absolutely wonderful! Our readers obviously sense this isn't just trendy psychobabble. It's something very effective and simple and real, and it actually makes people feel better. I think we're onto something here. Could you ask RSW whether she can send us more? And while you're at it, we really need to get her Social Security number and address so we can send her the standard paperwork. I understand the need for privacy and all that, but we do need to work through the proper channels. Just drop by my assistant's desk on the way out, and leave the information with her."

A fine mess, indeed. How will I get out of this one? I spent my whole life as a good, obedient Catholic girl who never told even the whitest of lies. Now I'm stuck in the proverbial web of deceit. I've wanted so badly for readers to love what I write, and now that's happened. Except it's not really me; it's RSW. Maybe I should come clean right now. It may be the easiest way. But what if Paige is horrified that I deceived her? I've heard she has a terrible temper if crossed. She may even fire me. How will I pay rent or buy groceries? The job market has really tightened up in the last year, especially for magazine writers. Oh, gawd, I'm in trouble!

"Well, I can see what she says. No problem, Paige. I'll check into it."

What am I doing? This is exactly what I don't want to say! Just tell her now, fool! Bite the bullet and confess.

"How many articles do you think RSW can send us? Do you want me to talk to her myself?"

"Uh, better not. Like I said, she's really weird – she's afraid of most people, but she trusts me. But maybe I can ask her to send a different 'empower' article once a month?"

"How can you be so sure she'll agree when you haven't spoken to her yet?"

Oh, what a tangled web we weave. How do I get out of this one?

"Well, I figured right away that this type of article would have some impact so I asked her about the possibility of writing others. Back then, she seemed interested in sending more."

"Despite what you've said about her, it actually sounds as if RSW is reliable and easy to work with. Have you met her? Do you have any idea what she looks like? Can you ask her to e-mail a picture to us so we can run it on our Web site?"

My mind is scrambling for excuses. I'm not good at this; I'm not used to lying. The last time I lied was when I told my ex-fiancé that he was the best I have ever slept with. And I did it just to boost his ego after his "wiener" died at the finish line.

"Oh, I haven't met her face to face. I can't imagine she would want her picture associated with the column; she really values her privacy. Like I've mentioned before, she has some kind of social phobias."

Paige looks as though she wants to press the issue but then decides not to.

"Hmph. It's strange that someone so troubled could write such profound and sensitive things. Still, I know how quirky creative people can be. Really, Annie, you should try reading the article as soon as you wake up in the morning. It's very powerful!"

Paige seems to be lost in her own fantasy about who RSW is. She has no clue that her precious new find is actually standing before her. If she knew, she would find a whole new use for Women & Co.'s 180-plus pages of high-end photography and slick, full-color advertising – as an effective tool in clubbing deceitful ex-employees across the head. I'm really cornered now. Damn it! I wish I'd attended the advanced media ethics class in college instead of sneaking off to drink beer and play cards with my guy friends.

"Do you think RSW could send another article sometime in the next week?"

"Oh, sure."

"I still can't believe you haven't met RSW personally. You know her so well. You seem to know her as well as you know yourself."

"That's the best thing about Internet friends. You never have to leave the house to connect. Well, talk to you later, Paige. I'll be sure to get that information to your assistant as soon as I can."

"OK, Annie. Let me know immediately when the next column arrives. Oh, and that look really works well for you. You should always wear color."

I mumble a quick thanks and run for the door. Better get out before I create a whole staff of imaginary dwarves who live with RSW and also want to write for the magazine: Tipsy, Blinky, Naughty, Mopey, Slutty, Haughty, Chunky and – in honor of Ashley – Nosy.

Speaking of the devil, Ashley is a few feet outside Paige's office, pretending to wait for a "very important" document to arrive over the fax.

"Psst, Annie..."

She stage-whispers so that only 20 or so co-workers can hear.

"So is it true? Is it actually true that Paige wants RSW to publish other articles?"

"How do you know?"

I struggle to hide my frustration. Ashley is definitely in the wrong business. This girl should be a private eye or a detective or a CIA agent. Except she could never keep a secret. Just chill, Annie, and remember to give your best to the world.

"Are you kidding? The entire editorial department knows about it. We have never received so many e-mails to one article. I'm dying to meet RSW. She's really helped me a lot."

"You're exaggerating. That article was published only three days ago."

"Remember Kevin, the guy I've been dating for the last nine months?"

"Yes."

"Well, I thought he was using me. When I read the article, I realized he wasn't using me. I was allowing myself to be with a man whom I felt was using me. You know what I'm saying?"

"And what has changed in your life?"

"Absolutely everything. When I read that article, I proclaimed out loud: "Starting today I empower myself to receive true love and to feel truly loved."

"And?"

"He called me to go out last night, and I said I would go out with him only if he wanted to date me."

I can't help myself from saying something mean.

"I bet you a hundred bucks that on the first rainy Friday that you feel lonely, you're going to run into his arms, right?"

"Yes, I am!"

"Wow, I see RSW helped you big time."

"Do you want to know why I would go out with him?"

Even if I don't, I know she's going to tell me.

"Why?"

"Because after I told him that, he drove to my house and asked whether I'd like to be his girlfriend. Like, his only girlfriend – strictly exclusive. He also said he didn't feel right that our relationship was just physical in the past and felt uncomfortable about it but was afraid to insist on something more serious. So now we're dating. Let me tell you, your friend RSW rocks."

My reputation in the editorial department has skyrocketed only for being RSW's friend. Before, they associated me with Citrus and Macadamia-Nut Cookies. Now, I'm known primarily as RSW's friend. That's what I call positive thinking.

As usual, Ashley takes my angry silence as an invitation to keep talking.

"I'd love to know where RSW lives. It can't be too hard to find out, with tools like the Internet and all those massive directories out there. I've solved much more complicated puzzles before."

Indeed, Ashley missed her true calling. She should be working as an investigator for the LAPD. You know what? I should practice some generosity and use Ashley's talent to help find Liz's daughter. Not only that, a challenge like this might help distract her from digging into this RSW mess.

"Ashley, I need to ask you for a favor. It's really important – strictly confidential."

This is all Ashley needs to hear. As I fill her in on Liz's story, I can see her eyes sparkle with excitement. She begins interrogating me for every little detail, then furiously taking notes. She's like a young retriever, lathering and pulling at the leash while someone fires a ball into the far-off brush.

Fabulous! This way she stays occupied, my work pays off, and I can have extra time to do my grocery shopping.

I love shopping after work because that's when I see "my people." You know, all the lonely people strolling down the aisles of the grocery store with no friends, no husband and no kids to take care of. Some of them might have a cat or a dog, as evidenced by the rawhide bones and bags of kibble in their carts. What a sad world. Lonely, isolated people pouring all their love and money into slobbering dogs and indifferent cats. Now, let me check out the list: Double Stuf Oreos, frozen pizza, chocolate chip ice cream, diet cola. Hey, stop! I need to practice kindness and generosity when it comes to food. I need to give the best to my body. Bye-bye, beloved sweets. If Cinderella discovers we're having an affair, I'm a dead woman. Yuck, I hate this! I want my sweet and salt and junk food. Poor me. Be strong, Annie Joseph! You're doing all this for your career. And I may need some knock-out clips in my portfolio after Paige discovers the whole RSW fiasco and fires me.

Wow, what was that terrific noise? Oh my! That poor guy knocked over that whole pyramid of tomato sauce cans. Yikes. That's normally something I would do. Oh no, Cinderella is whispering in my ear again, that little pest. Ugh, guess I should try to do the right thing and ask him whether he needs help. All right, here's the magic word to motivate me: unemployment. Just jump in and do it.

"Hi, do you need help?"

"I …"

I don't believe this! It's Ben, whose designer shirt I cleverly accessorized with coffee a couple of weeks ago. Here I am, being a Good Samaritan to the man who's probably making spaghetti sauce for his latest bimbo du jour.

"What a coincidence! It's the 'jovial Annie' from *Women and Co*. What a small world."

He remembered my name. How about that? Then again, how could he forget the woman who gave him a hot coffee bath? Oh, Lord … I'm shaking. I need to settle down or he'll think I have Parkinson's. If this guy makes me feel like I'm 15 when he's across the room, can you imagine how I feel when he's two inches away from me?

"Yes, it's me."

"I'll never forget the look of horror when you spilled that coffee on me. Wish I'd had a camera to capture it; it was kind of charming, actually. Do you always come to this supermarket?"

"Yes, I live close by."

Wow. I'm just filled with scintillating conversation. Silence. Three seconds of excruciating, horrifying silence. I need to start a conversation immediately. How about asking him whether the cucumbers are hard? Oops, maybe not a good idea. I can feel my whole face flushing red – as red as the labels on the cans of sauce surrounding us.

"So, you were buying tomato sauce, right?"

Oh, jovial Annie, you're obviously the sharpest knife in the drawer. Stay green with envy all you amoebas, as you witness my amazing feats of conversational brilliance!

"Yes, and you just found out that I'm clumsy."

"You're no worse than I am; your poor shirt is evidence of that."

He chuckles – a nice, masculine sound.

"That's why I wasn't too hard on you; I've done things much more embarrassing than that. I've already knocked down so many displays in this store that I think the manager dispatches a stockboy to trail me whenever they see me enter. Speaking of which, here comes someone to pick up the rest of them."

Ha, ha, ha. Cute little joke, not funny; at least it will allow me to smile and slowly move toward the cashier. Please Ben, don't come to the same register. I can't stand in line with you and try to think of interesting conversation. Thank goodness I didn't fill my cart with tampons or Vagisil or the usual array of fattening junk food. He should be impressed by all the organic stuff. And it looks like I'm not going to lose him anytime soon – he's getting in line right behind me.

"You know, I miss the days when Mom cooked special meals for us. I miss the smell of pasta and sauce simmering in the kitchen. Pasta with tomato sauce and basil..."

Aha! Gotcha! I knew it! For him, the Brady Bunch's mom was a real woman! It was simply a matter of time before you showed your true colors, mister. You're surely hoping for the day when you can get your very own Stepford wife, all pretty with her cute apron on, waiting for her man to come into their immaculate home where a perfectly cooked candlelight dinner awaits. With pasta "al dente." Still, I can't help but humor the guy. He's so gorgeous, it's a treat just being seen talking to him.

"Yes, some things are hard to let go. But I'm sure your wife cooks a lot of gourmet macaroni and cheese with tomato sauce and basil."

Oops, can't help my big mouth!

"Unfortunately, there's nobody waiting for me with my favorite meal on the table. That's not what I really want from a woman. All I want is someone to love and who loves me back. Isn't that what we all want?"

I can't believe he's telling me this! Here we stand in the least romantic spot on earth – with the unflattering fluorescent lights and the high school cashier snapping her gum and the signs that say kumquats are on sale – and this man, this beautiful man, is pouring out his heart to me. I hope there's someone behind me, because I'm about to pass out. Oh, gawd, how I want to run to his arms, smother him with kisses and spend the rest of my life making pasta for him. All within the next three minutes. Wow, this is a first. I've never wanted the cashier to take forever to price-check something, but I want to stand here, with Ben, forever. OK, get a grip, Annie Joseph. Ben doesn't even look at you as a woman. Obviously, you're just the cute, chubby, unthreatening colleague he feels so comfortable with that he'll tell anything to. What's that booming sound? Oh great. It's not a drive-by shooting – it's thunder. It definitely is pouring out there. Bad-hair alert. Ben doesn't look anxious to run out into the deluge either.

"That's some storm. Annie, is your car here in the parking lot? The grocery store has a nice little coffee shop. Why don't we wait it out there until it lets up a bit? Or, is someone waiting for you with an open apron?"

Tomorrow's headline: "Stunned fat lady assaults unsuspecting hunk by crushing him in her massive arms." Who would believe me if I told them HE invited me to have coffee? It's like a movie. In a couple of minutes, everyone's going to break into a song and tap dance down the aisles while Ben and I kiss passionately by the cash register. Annie Joseph, aren't you getting a little carried away? It's a cup of coffee. He probably just wants to protect his perfectly tousled hair and needs to while away the time with someone he finds vaguely pleasant. Tomorrow morning, he won't even remember my name. I'll be the ugly duckling – the homely, unintentionally amusing friend – among Ben's bevy of Barbies.

"No, there's no one waiting for me back home. Let's go have coffee."

"Great!"

We talk about everything there is to talk about. We start with awkward conversation about the weather and traffic, but completely bond after discovering we both had been deceived by our exes. From that point on, the conversation flows like we are old friends. Before I know it, it's midnight at the all-night supermarket. The rain dried up hours ago. We say our good-byes, but nothing else happens. No singing or dancing. Not even a good-night kiss. Even so, it's the best night I've had in the last 10 years. I have no clue what tomorrow will bring. I don't even want to know (you know I'm lying, right?). Today is all I need in my memory. When I get home to my empty apartment, I don't even turn on the TV or raid the fridge. Instead, I grab a pen and paper and jot down what turns out to be RSW's second article.

AS OF TODAY I EMPOWER MYSELF...

... TO GIVE PEOPLE MY BEST SMILE, EVEN IF I MAY NOT GET ONE BACK ...

... TO LOOK MY BEST AND PRESENT THE BEST IMAGE TO THE WORLD, EVEN IF I FEEL UNATTRACTIVE, DOWN AND BLOATED ...

... TO ALWAYS DECLARE WORDS OF JOY, EVEN IF I FEEL SAD AND DISAPPOINTED ...

... TO BE GENEROUS, EVEN IF I RECEIVE NOTHING IN RETURN ...

... TO OFFER THE BEST OF MYSELF EVERY DAY, NOT BECAUSE I AM TRYING TO PRETEND TO BE SOMEONE I AM NOT...

... BUT BECAUSE I WILL GIVE MYSELF PERMISSION TO EXPRESS TO THE WORLD THE BEST I CAN BE.

Chapter 6

Cinderella: A Warrior or a Medieval Barbie?

I'm *at the association's third meeting – or my body is, anyway. Mentally, I'm preoccupied with my new, favorite pastime – obsessing over Ben. I haven't seen him since our grocery store encounter. I keep thinking about our coffee talk, turning over all the details in my mind. Was it my imagination that he seemed to smile and laugh at everything I said, as if he found me quite charming? Were his weary comments about the dating scene just polite conversation – something single people say to each other – or did I sense a real loneliness, a craving for something more permanent in his life? Maybe after dating all those long-legged, vacant blondes, he finally discovered that "something" was me. Wake up, honey, it's just infatuation. An embarrassing schoolgirl's crush that you're much too old for. Must focus on something else, like the fact I've even lost a few pounds without having to count calories.*

"Hi, Annie. How've you been?"

"I'm doing great, Liz. How about you?"

"I'm fine, giving the world my absolute best. That's why I brought you a slice of organic banana cake, made with whole wheat and honey. Only the best for you, my dear."

"Wow! Thank you so much. It smells delicious, but if you keep spoiling me like this, they're going to have to haul me to these meetings in a crane. Say, Liz, I wanted to mention something. I talked to a journalist friend of mine recently, and she's going to try to find your daughter. I can't promise you anything, but we're going to give it a shot."

Liz's blue eyes fill with grateful tears.

"Oh, honey, that's wonderful! But I didn't make these sweets for you so I could get something in return."

"I know, Liz, I know. I just wanted to do this for you."

"You're such a sweetheart."

Liz suddenly looks very frail and tiny, and the tears are threatening to spill down her kind, lined face. But she blinks them away and quickly changes the subject.

"Annie, dear, you look great! Have you lost weight? There's a sparkle in your eyes. Wait a minute – you're in love!"

I can't believe this woman. Just like my own Nana, she seems to see right into my soul.

"No, no, not at all. Far from it."

Liz isn't buying my act.

"Hmmm. But some man has been catching your attention?"

"Well, maybe that's true; but, really, nothing's going on."

She looks triumphant.

"Aha, I knew it! I had the same look when I met my husband."

"I don't think my 'look' has anything to do with this guy. We spoke only once. He probably doesn't even remember my name."

"That's what you think. Today you gals may be more modern and aggressive than my generation, but love never changes. When Cupid's arrow hits you, it's always the same, no matter how old you are. My husband and I laid eyes on each other for the first time at City Hall. He asked me whether he could stay in touch through letters – that was back when people actually wrote letters, you know. He lived in another state. After being my pen pal for a whole year and talking on the phone just a few times, he came to see me. And he proposed."

"You decided to marry your husband after seeing him only once? That's absolutely crazy! You didn't even know whether you were compatible."

"That's right!"

Liz gets a faraway look in her eyes.

"Testing compatibility is sheer nonsense. I laugh whenever I see those online matchmaking services advertised on TV. You people think too much. Your heart is always right. Just listen to it. It will never deceive you. The moment I laid eyes on Bill, I felt my heart jump. That was my first indication he was the man I'd spend my life with. We were still happy after 35 years of marriage. We went through some hard times after Natalie left the house. But I loved that man until the day he died. I still love him and think of him every day."

"How nice. It's so refreshing to hear such incredible love stories."

"I think women nowadays are satisfied with so little; they just don't allow themselves to receive the best. Everything is so much faster. You know what I mean, right?"

Aha, I think she's trying to tactfully tell me that younger women are sluts.

"I understand, Liz. I understand."

"Don't get me wrong! I'm not against it, but I think the man first has to show us his best so we can judge whether he deserves our heart. Because our heart lives inside our body, it's something sacred. So we have to give our sacred body to the one who truly deserves it."

Sacred body? Liz, your romantic outlook is really sweet and old-fashioned, but give me a break!

"How could you judge whether your husband deserved your heart after meeting him only once?"

"After exchanging letters for 11 months, he came to my house to ask for my hand in marriage. As soon as he got there, we sat in the backyard to talk. I had the strongest craving for passion fruit, but it wasn't in season. So he jumped in his car and drove miles and miles until he found a tiny market that carried passion fruit. He came back to my home with a big smile on his face and a truckload of the stuff. At that moment I knew that he would do anything to make me happy."

"What a great story, Liz. Love is such a mystery. And way more mysterious is the way people choose their 'love.' "

Wow! I don't even sound like myself.

"If you really like this young man, then before you give him your heart and your body, make sure he would bring you passion fruit. Oops! Not 'passion fruit' – that's not what I am trying to say – but that he would do anything to make you happy."

"I'll never forget your advice, Liz."

Cathy enters the room. Dressed in a tasteful celery-green suit, she's as perfectly coiffed and perpetually cheerful as an aging beauty queen. This is weird – I'm kind of looking forward to this next session.

"Good evening to you all! I hope you have benefited from these meetings so far. Some people may have had more difficulty than others, but the important thing is to not stop practicing and to observe the results. Before we start with our next teaching, let's go over a wonderful passage in Cinderella's story."

" '... On a certain occasion, the king had a ball. He invited all the women in the kingdom so his son could choose a young lady to marry.

" 'There was general excitement. Cinderella wanted to go, but her stepmother enforced three conditions: that she complete all her chores, that she help her stepsisters get ready first, and that she find or make her own dress. Determined, Cinderella finished all her work, helped her stepsisters get dressed and found a dress in a trunk that belonged to her mother. After cleverly stitching remnants of her stepsisters' dresses to this dress, she was ready to go to the ball.' "

Here we go again.

"In this passage we can spot a distinct characteristic of heroes and heroines: the determination and effort to fulfill their dreams. Cinderella had a dream: to temporarily escape the drudgery of her life and go to the ball. In this moment of the story, she didn't wait for her Prince Charming to knock on her door. She didn't know he existed at that time. She just focused on one thing: Going to the ball was her goal, and she worked hard to achieve it. And now based on this part of the story, I want to ask you something: What have you done to make your dreams come true?"

Predictably, Steve is first to attack. I've decided he absolutely must be doing an investigative piece. I notice he's wearing better clothes, but surely that shirt isn't his best.

"Cathy, when we don't have 'the luck' or the 'fate' of a Cinderella, it's not easy to achieve our dreams."

Now let's see how you handle this one, Happy Cathy. I swing around, almost certain she will have a good answer.

"You're right, Steve. A lot of people don't fulfill their dreams mainly because they don't believe it's possible to do it. That's the problem. Some people don't allow themselves to accept their real dreams and live vicariously through other people's dreams. The Greek philosopher Epictetus said that if you strongly want what is not yours, you end up losing what is yours. They are heroes who never give up a goal because they believe they can do it and nothing discourages them."

"Cathy, I'm still not clear on this. Could you explain it a little further?"

"Of course, Beatrice. Heroes and heroines don't question their dreams, they see their dreams as a calling for their true path. They just accept them and try to fulfill them. Mainly because they know that it's in this fulfillment that they can find success and a reason for their existence. They're also aware that they're not alone in this search for fulfillment. They know the *Grand Life* does everything to help them."

"The *Grand Life*? This sounds a little too religious for me."

"Steve, when I say *Grand Life*, I'm referring to a power that encourages human beings to find their absolute fulfillment. Some say this power comes from a Higher Power, be it God, the Universe, the angels or even fairies. If this explanation offends you because it's too religious, then I can quote some famous researchers of human behavior, such as Maslow and Carl Rogers. Through their research, they learned that, even in an unhealthy environment, plants seek sun and life. Similarly, human beings, even under adverse conditions, have an inner strength that propels them to grow to their full potential. Rogers discovered that all life forms are moved by a natural inclination to develop their full potential to advance their growth. This predisposition, this power that encourages us to develop the best in us, is what I call the *Grand Life*."

"All right, so what does Cinderella have to do with it all?"

Steve has a scowl that suggests he could storm out of the room at any moment.

"In this story, the ball symbolizes Cinderella's dream, the desires of her soul, the cause of her work and effort. Some people can interpret the fulfillment of her dream as the result of a magic trick. The fairy godmother appears and with the touch of her magic wand, she makes Cinderella's dreams come true."

"It's clear that she did nothing for the fairy godmother to appear and fulfill her wishes."

Steve looks for support, but to me he seems petulant rather than triumphant.

"What I'm trying to show you is another interpretation of that same story. I'm not saying I'm 100 percent right. I just want to present to you another viewpoint. You don't have to agree with me, just allow yourselves to become familiar with it."

"And what's the other viewpoint?"

This Cathy never ceases to amaze me. Despite Steve's constant objections, she remains as serene as the Dalai Lama.

"Steve, as I said before, I believe the *Grand Life* is the force that gives human beings the drive to develop their potential and achieve their goals. As the laws of physics explain, every force moves in a definite direction, right?"

"Right."

"When we walk in the *Grand Life's* direction, we're walking in the direction of realizing our dreams."

"In which direction is this supposed *Grand Life* moving?"

"When observing the development of a plant, researchers of human behavior noticed that this force, this *Grand Life*, always moves toward growth, toward creation. So if we want to go along with this force, we need to move in the same direction. Like I mentioned in our last meeting, instead of complaining and allowing negative thoughts to bring her down, Cinderella decided to act like a heroine, work hard and develop constructive attitudes. This way she was in sync with the *Grand Life*. When we walk in the *Grand Life's* direction, we walk toward growth, toward creation. That way our strength and our life improve. I believe that the fairy godmother didn't come out of nowhere in Cinderella's life.

She was attracted by Cinderella's heroic attitude, which was in agreement with the *Grand Life*."

"I'm sorry. All this sounds too much like a New Age fairy tale for me. It doesn't sound like anything I can apply to real life. How can I walk in the *Grand Life's* direction?"

I'm starting to wish I'd met Steve earlier. I could have taken him to all the press conferences for new restaurant openings so I would only have to open my mouth in the end during the sample tasting.

Although Steve is working mightily to push Cathy's buttons, she never loses composure. In fact, this has become my new game: "Will Today Be the Day Steve Makes Cathy Blow Her Stack?" I grin just thinking of it.

"When we develop a 'heroic' attitude, we help the *Grand Life* to work and show the way to our complete fulfillment. For the *Grand Life* to help fulfill your dreams, you need first to accept your true dreams, because as I mentioned before, your dreams are a door to your true path. Now I ask you, Steve, what is your greatest dream? Within every hero's or heroine's heart beats strong wishes. You can ignore them, give up trying to fulfill them or believe it's not worth trying. But they're there waiting to be fulfilled."

And what is so "heroic" about wanting to go to a royal ball? I assume Cathy wants me to fulfill my dream by knocking on a publisher's door with one hand while holding my storybook in the other. Does she really think it's that easy to break into the publishing market? I'd like to see how Cinderella would handle my situation. Yeah, she'd get out of the limo in her Prada dress, knock on their door and expect the publisher to give her a book contract because she's pretty and, by the way, can scrub floors. This silly talk is getting on my last nerve. I'd rather think about whether Ben would drive all over the country searching for passion fruit for me.

I'd give anything to be a fly on the wall so I could see what Ben is doing at this very moment. I'm sure he's doing something way more fun than I am. He's probably in the arms of a gorgeous woman with pink Gucci shoes, flirting like crazy.

"Nowhere in the story does Cinderella think her desire to go to the ball is hopeless, or that she won't be able to come up with a fabulous dress. She's not giving up or feeling unable to fulfill her dream. Do you let yourselves accept your dreams and wishes? Or do you keep finding excuses such as: 'That's not for me,' 'My family isn't rich,' or 'Good things happen only to other people'?"

Steve, you've never been able to keep your mouth shut before. Go for it, buddy. Please say something now! He does.

"Many people declare their dream to the world, but they don't achieve their dreams. Just acknowledging our dreams is not enough."

"Absolutely, Steve. We know it's not enough to dream. You have to work like Cinderella did. Even the prince, who had it all, had to go knock on every door to find his princess. What if you had the crystal slipper in your hand to find what you want? You've met your princess and now you need to knock on every door. How many people do you think would completely give it up as hopeless? As a more practical example, how many people want to start their own business, but give up thinking they don't have enough money or knowledge to do it? A lot of people just give up without even doing the work: knocking on every door until they find what they want."

"It all sounds very nice and all, but I just can't believe that work alone will make our dreams come true. I know many people who work very hard, and they don't feel that they live a truly fulfilled life."

Hallelujah, Brother Steve. That's the story of my life. I work myself into a frenzy, yet no prince has ever knocked on my door with a crystal slipper in one hand and passion fruit in the other.

"You are right, Steve, working hard is just one part of the process to following our dream. The other is walking and living like heroes and heroines so we can attract the help of the *Grand Life.* And when we work hard to achieve our dreams, we become a force. When we connect with the

Grand Life, we become a potential. We need to grow from the outside, but we can't forget to grow on the inside. You can have a successful career, work hard to develop ways to manage thousands of employees and forget to develop ways to have a good relationship with the members of your own family. If you choose this path, you can achieve material success but you are not a hero, you are not connected with the *Grand Life*. In these meetings I hope you can learn tools to become a hero and have it all."

Beatrice stands to join the naysayers.

"And Cinderella fits into all this ... how?"

"Beatrice, at this point in the story, the only thing Cinderella desires is to go to the ball, and she works hard to make it happen. We know that she not only succeeds at getting to the ball, but she also does much more – she becomes a princess. She didn't become a princess by the touch of a magic wand. While working to fulfill her dream of going to the ball, even though she wasn't aware of it, she was preparing for a greater mission. Cinderella didn't become nobility by marrying her prince. She attracted the prince by her "noble attitude." Even during the hard times while she was scrubbing the floors, she was not only working to fulfill her dream of going to the ball but she also was developing noble values such as humility, dedication, determination – all virtues worthy of a true princess! She didn't know she was working to become a princess, and yet, all this while, the *Grand Life* was helping her become one."

This talk about the Grand Life is getting way too metaphysical. Could somebody say something soon? Steve? Are you awake? Beatrice is.

"And what can we do for the *Grand Life* to help us?"

"There's an example in the Bible of how the *Grand Life* influences a true hero's path. In everyone's eyes, David was a simple little shepherd in the hills of Bethlehem, but for the *Grand Life* he had the potential to be the man who would defeat Goliath and become king. In Cinderella and David's stories, we can spot a trait that is inherent to true heroes and heroines. When David was a simple shepherd and Cinderella was doing domestic work, you never heard them complain: "Man, this is such a drag! Why doesn't anyone notice what a great job I'm doing?" They were filled with humility, and wanted only to do well at what was before them. Imagine what it's like to do a job that is not respected by others, a job that's considered simple. Imagine how it feels to have barely any possessions beyond the rags or hides on your back. Cinderella had only an old dress to go to the ball, and David didn't have impressive armor to fight against the giant Goliath. But like heroes, they heard their calling, allowed themselves to follow the desires of their hearts and succeeded in fulfilling their wishes. All of this without the appropriate connections, material goods or supplies."

"And what does all this mean, Cathy?"

It's the first time I've heard Liz say anything during a meeting. Poor thing, she looks terrified. All this must be very confusing for her. All right, I confess: It's confusing for me too! It's hard to confess, even more so when I'm a reporter who is expected to understand a variety of complex world issues, read at least three newspapers a day and most of the popular magazines, and be plugged into everything from "YouTube" to "The Office" to "Hardball with Chris Matthews." Even at a "women's magazine," where you'd think you need only a working knowledge of how to apply lip gloss, I've found it useful to have a broad body of knowledge; you just never know what you'll have to write about. I mean, look at me sitting here, listening to fairy tales. Whew! Here I am in my own little, self-absorbed world. Better shift focus back to the meeting. Otherwise the only thing I'll have to face is the pressure of finding a new job.

"Good question, Liz."

Cathy raises her eyebrows and smiles.

"What I mean to say is that the part the *Grand Life* plays in fulfilling our calling materializes through us: wherever we are, with whatever we have and whoever we are. The best way the *Grand Life* can help us is when we empower ourselves to be the best we can be in the moment we are. Each person's path is unique. It's no use wanting to wear anyone else's armor or dress. Heroes value themselves. They know they can find their fulfillment exactly where they are at that point in time. Even if you feel you are in a situation in which you will never achieve your dreams, instead of giving up, act like a hero and just embrace where you are. Give your best and continue to dream, because maybe you don't know what to do to make your dreams come true, but the *Grand Life* will find a way. So from now on, we'll put this into practice: Work hard to achieve where you want to be, and give your best and be grateful for where you are."

Cathy turns the board and her words are up there in that same perfect script. Liz speaks again, her brow furrowed.

"What do you mean by doing our best?"

"The best in you, not by trying to be someone else. In the next couple of weeks, get in touch with your true dreams – those desires of your soul – and try to work toward achieving them. What are your strengths and values? What is important to you? As you know, important means necessary. It comes from the word *import, to bring*. So ask yourselves: What do I want to bring into my life? What is necessary for me to be happy? What's important to me? This week, allow yourselves to dream and free your deepest desires. And give your best and do your best to make those dreams come true. Your boss may not appreciate your work; your companion may not see your true value. You may feel you lack the necessary supplies, contacts or money to succeed. Yet, never abandon your true dreams because you think you don't have the ideal situation. Remember that you're not alone in this journey; the *Grand Life* is helping you along the way. The *Grand Life* doesn't care where you are now. It cares about where you're going. See you soon."

I leave the meeting more discouraged than ever. I even ignore my doorman when he tells me he has the package with the DVDs for which I've been waiting for weeks. Without warning, I find tears streaming down my cheeks. I start to wonder what is really important in my life and what I am doing to fulfill the desires of my soul. Truth is, I haven't even allowed myself to dream. At one point in my life, I just lost hope and lived on "autopilot." Then I just worked to make other people's dreams come true.

I can't let myself enjoy the simplest of things. I watch a romantic movie and just when I'm about to cry, I hear a voice in my head telling me how ridiculous the plot is. Every time I've dared to think of taking my collection of short stories to a publisher, I give up. Why? Because I tell myself "a lot of people more talented than you don't get published because they can't find agents or publishers." But really, this is not a law. It's a self-defeating thought in my head, a limit I choose to place on myself. I think of Ben 27 hours a day, but when Liz asks about him, I act as if it's no big deal. Who do I think I'm fooling? And what the hell am I doing with my life? The important things in my life have become ice cream and cold cuts and TV! I want to get married really badly, yet I believe all the stuff, even the stuff in our own stupid magazine that claims marriage is an outdated institution. I'm dying to see my father, yet I keep saying I don't really miss him. It just hurts to be me! I want to cry and so finally I do.

Late that night, after I've wept through half a box of Kleenex and tired of staring at "Sex in the City" reruns, I begin to reassess things. Maybe these realizations aren't so bad. You know what? From now on, I'll empower myself to work hard to achieve what's really important to me. I'll start looking for a publisher tomorrow. I'll come to terms with my dream to get married and nurture friendships. I'll change. Oh, gawd, what if I fail? Well, I'm not going to think about that; the only important thing for a "heroine" – if I must use Cathy's terminology – is to empower herself to work hard to fulfill her dreams. The outcome doesn't matter at this point. "The Grand Life" – ugh, there I go again – knows why these dreams are in my heart.

Wake up, Annie Joseph. First of all, you don't know anyone at a publishing house. Second of all, you barely take care of your three little plants. What makes you think you can take care of a whole family? Whatever!

You know what? I'm not going to wait till tomorrow. I'm going to start right now. I'm going to click off the TV, park myself in front of the computer and start a new article for RSW.

AS OF TODAY, I EMPOWER MYSELF …

… TO ACCEPT MY TRUE DESIRES.

… TO FEEL THE LONGINGS THAT BEAT IN MY HEART.

… TO BE ACQUAINTED WITH MY DEEPEST EMOTIONS.

… TO WAKE UP MY TALENTS AND POTENTIAL.

… TO WORK TOWARD FULFILLING MY DREAMS.

… TO ALLOW MYSELF TO FIND MY PATH.

… TO VALUE WHAT I HAVE AND WHO I AM...

… TO HAVE THE COURAGE TO RECOGNIZE WHAT IS IMPORTANT IN MY LIFE.

… TO NOT COMPARE MYSELF TO OTHERS NOR TO BRING MYSELF DOWN.

… BECAUSE BEING TRUE TO MYSELF IS THE ONLY WAY THAT I CAN LISTEN TO THE VOICE OF MY HIDDEN SOUL.

Chapter 7

If Only I Could be Sleeping Beauty

The first thing I do this morning is call several publishing houses to try to make an appointment to pitch my book. After a disheartening string of "No, not interested," I finally connect with someone at a small publishing house who says she'll review my manuscript. It is so refreshing to hear this glimmer of promise after a sleepless night filled with anxious thoughts. During the next month, I have to make what's important to me come true: the publishing of my book. This week I'm going to devote myself to re-reading and refining the stories. I'll do everything in my power to make my dream come true. No more leaving my dream in a dark closet. The thought of unveiling my "baby" gives me butterflies in my stomach. However, I'm not alone. As Cathy says, "The 'Grand Life' is helping me as we speak." I know Cinderella is proud of me.

But first things first. I've got a lot of research to do for my Cinderella project. I've already done exhaustive research on the origins of fairy tales and what they mean to each culture. I've talked to several prominent psychologists about the basic principles of the group. Although all of them found the "fairy tale" book to be unconventional, they seemed to believe the seminars were based on sound psychological research. In fact, one of the experts, a Dr. H. Wolf, gave me a fabulous quote:

"Without having the benefit of attending these self-improvement seminars myself, I can say they seem to represent a fairly positive and grounded viewpoint. It sounds as though they generally want people to approach life with healthier expectations and a more positive outlook, while not staying entrenched in the past. That's certainly something any reputable mental-health practitioner would try to encourage his or her patients to do. And if it's actually true that this underground society doesn't profit monetarily from its teachings, that's also encouraging. While I wouldn't recommend people use a group such as this as a substitute for professional help, I can see how it would supplement their recovery toward wellness. At the very least, it wouldn't hurt anyone to participate."

Finding out about the actual society has been trickier. Conventional media has written nothing. Paige wasn't kidding when she called it an underground phenomenon. Thank goodness for blogs. I've found several glowing reports from people who claim their lives were transformed by a "secret fairy tale society." So my first priority after arriving at the office this morning is to contact one of the bloggers. As if by magic, Ashley bounces around the corner to interrupt my train of thought. How does she always get to work before I do? I'm beginning to think she sleeps under the copier.

"Annie, I have good news – and great news! Which do you want to hear first?"

"The great news, please."

"OK. It's about your friend's missing daughter. After doing a lot of research, I think I finally tracked her down."

"Really? Did you talk to her?"

"No, I thought it would be better if you did that."

"This is fantastic. Give me all the information. I'll call her right now. On second thought, it's still early. I should wait a while. Maybe I should call her later this afternoon. OK, what's the good news?"

"You won't believe this! You know Ben? Beautiful Ben? He popped his head into our cubicle early this morning, and he was actually looking for you!"

At the sound of Ben's name, my heart starts beating as if it belongs to a hyper-caffeinated hummingbird. I struggle to maintain composure, as if hunky men routinely pop into our office to inquire about me. Play it cool, Annie.

"What did you tell him?"

"That I didn't know whether you were in yet or were maybe on an early-morning assignment. Oh, and I asked him whether he wanted your cell number."

God bless Ashley. She's a snoop and a pain, but she thinks of everything.

"And he said?"

Ashley smiles proudly and my heart leaps.

"I didn't even wait for him to answer me. I just gave him your number. Did you go out with him already?"

"Me? Go out with him? No, no, no. We're just friends, you know, nothing beyond that."

She gives me a highly skeptical look but, for once, doesn't press the issue. Annie Joseph, you sweet little moron! Now the whole editorial department will know not only that you have the hots for Ben but also that you religiously read Cosmo's "Gossip" section. Could you come up with more of a cliché? "We're just friends?" Ugh, what was I thinking? Let us pray: Dear Angels, Fairies, Elves, "Grand Life" – anyone who isn't too busy – please have Ben call me! What does he want? Oh, the joy, the anxiety, the fear, the sexual yearning. Did I just say sexual yearning? Wow! I said the "S" word – even if only to myself. Does anybody have some Super Glue? My cell phone and I are going to be cemented together, like Siamese twins.

"Oh, Annie, and one more thing: Gabrielle wants to talk to you."

"Gabrielle? As in Gabrielle from 'Everyday Heroines'?"

Silly me. What other woman in the building has such a delicate and ethereal name? I can't figure out why Miss Universe, who never gave me the time of day, now wants to talk to me. Maybe she's Ben's old girlfriend so she wants to engage me in an electric stapler duel while screaming "Bloody whore!" So here I am, back in high school, the wannabe slutty girl. Why do I feel my vocabulary belongs in the sewer? Why do I keep thinking negatively about myself? I take a few deep breaths and head to Gabrielle's cubicle.

"Hi, Gabrielle. You wanted to see me?"

"Yes, Annie. As you've probably heard, I'm getting married next week. Well, I wanted to make sure to extend a personal invitation to the wedding. It's been so crazy that I forgot to ask you earlier!"

"Sure, I understand. Thanks for the invitation. And congratulations, by the way."

Isn't it weird that she invited me? I'd heard the buzz that she was getting married, but I never thought she'd invite me – the lowly food writer. I wonder what she wants from me?

"Oh, Annie, one more thing: Do you think you could talk RSW into giving me her e-mail? It'd be great if you could. It seems everyone – myself included – just loves her articles. I'd love to give her some positive feedback on her work. Paige told me she suffers from some kind of social phobia. How fascinating! That could make for a great article. You know, if she'd really open up and talk about it, she might be able to help so many people out there. Everyone seems to respect her so much. I'd love to write an article on her, her beliefs – everything!"

"Hmmm, that might be hard. She's very stubborn on things like this. But I'll try my best."

OK, now we're talking. She didn't invite Annie Joseph; she invited RSW. RSW is special, not Annie Joseph. But as the only person who "knows" her, I'm enjoying popularity by association. As if I need another reminder of this monster I've created. Thankfully, no one has pestered me about RSW's true identity lately. For once, I'm relieved that Oasis – the mega-corporation that publishes Women & Co., Men & Co., and a half-dozen other magazines – recently installed a massive payment system, which has proven to be as complex and bug-ridden as it is expensive. For one nightmarish pay period in November, it issued paychecks for $12.32 to everyone in the research department, while doubling the salaries of all mail-room employees. This certainly should make it easier to somehow lose the Social Security number and personal information of a new freelance columnist, just one of Oasis' hundreds of freelance contributors. And as long as RSW doesn't call to complain that her check was lost, everything should be OK. Well, for a while, anyway.

I'd better get back to my desk and try to at least look busy. I reach into my purse for my cell and flip it open. Is this a mirage or is the red light blinking? Why, oh why, did I separate from my precious Siamese twin for a couple of minutes? Why does this always happen? It never fails. When you want something really badly, it slips through your fingers, but when you let it go, it happens. Oh, blessed fairy godmother, touch the phone with your magic wand and make the call from Ben! Please don't let it be a telemarketer, a bill collector or the super from my building calling to tell me they had to fog for roaches again. If it's a message from Ben, I promise I'll give away little statues of Cinderella, create a Cinderella fan club and write chain letters proclaiming: "If you send the sentence 'I love Cinderella' to 10 of your friends, your dreams will be fulfilled."

"Hi Annie, this is Ben. Remember? From the supermarket? Well, when you have a moment, please call me. Later!"

Ecstatic, I push the message button again, just to hear the sound of his low, sexy voice.

"Hi, Annie, this is Ben. Remember? From the supermarket? Well, when you have a moment, please call me. Later!"

Remember? As if I've thought of anyone else. As if I run into gorgeous men at the supermarket all the time. A compulsive desire to listen to his message 257 times overpowers me! Oh-my-gawd. B-E-N actually called ME! He wants to talk to ME – the former nobody food writer. I can't get over it! He has such a smooth, sexy voice. OK, just one more time. Please don't judge me because I'm crazy. When a sexy man calls someone like me, the moment must be preserved forever.

"Hi, Annie, this is Ben. Remember? From the supermarket? Well, when you have a moment, please call me. Later!"

OK, I absolutely, positively swear this will be the last time. "Hi Annie, this is Ben ..."

Somebody help me. I can't stop listening to this message! I need the number to VAA (Voicemail Addicts Anonymous). I might as well give up getting any real research done today. I'll just have to fake work. That means looking very professional and busy, even while I'm mooning over Ben. Should I call now or wait? I feel as nervous as a teenager, but the suspense is killing me. So now I'm scrambling through the junk in my top drawer for the company directory, my hands shaking as I locate his name. Take a deep breath, Annie. You can do this. Now I'm dialing the number. The phone is ringing, ringing, ringing. I'm just about to hang up when I hear his voice on the other end.

"Oh, hi. Ben? I thought your voicemail was going to pick up."

"Hi, Annie!"

Is it my imagination or does he sound genuinely happy to hear from me? He speaks.

"I was just stepping away from my desk but picked up when I remembered it might be you. How's everything going?"

"Oh, great, great."

"I was wondering whether you wanted to do lunch today?"

"Great."

"So, how about we meet at that new restaurant – what is it, Grady's? – right across the street from the office?"

"Great."

"Does one o'clock work for you?"

"Great."

I hang up, shuddering at my conversational skills. He's going to think I took some cut-rate "Learn English by Mail" course and learned only how to say "great." But it doesn't matter. I'm the happiest woman in the world. Just then, the phone rings again. Maybe it's Ben and he's changed his mind. Hurriedly, I pick up the receiver and, in my most professional voice, announce Women & Co. Except this time it's my father's unmistakable baritone.

"Hello, Annie? Is Annie there?"

I (unconvincingly) disguise my voice, tell him Annie is not there and hang up. I'm also surprised to find tears flowing down my cheeks. Why am I crying, just because my father called? He has been calling for years, and I never felt this way. A part of me wants to forget everything he did to hurt me and start talking to him again, but right now that is a mountain I can't climb. My tears stop short when Ashley speaks up.

"Annie, was that your father? Good grief. How badly did that man hurt you?"

"Never mind,"

I mutter something else, then blow into a tissue.

But I mind. This week I need to empower myself to recognize what's really important to me. I miss my dad a lot, but let's face it: I can't forgive him. If I do, it's like I'm saying all the pain he caused is forgotten. It's like saying it didn't matter, when it did.

"I'm sorry, Ashley. I do mind. I lied when I said it didn't matter. I miss my dad a lot, but he hurt me big time."

"What did he do, Annie? Did he abuse you? You know, stuff like that?"

I can't believe I'm about to pour my heart out to Ashley, but I'm tired of keeping this painful secret.

"No, not at all. He left my mom for another woman. When my mother got sick, I had to take care of her by myself. He hardly ever called us. He only mailed the alimony and sent me Christmas and birthday gifts. Then Mom passed away. He separated from 'the other woman' and decided he wanted to be a dad again. So he started to call me. But you know what? Too late. When I needed him, he didn't even call. It's not easy. It's very painful. You have to understand – I adored my dad; he was my hero. We had some really good times together. I just can't get over the fact that he abandoned me at a time when I needed him most. To make it worse, he chose another woman over his real family."

Ashley's eyes are filled with genuine sympathy.

"Annie, he separated from your mother, not from you."

"I'm sorry Ashley, but only someone who has experienced something like this can understand what I'm going through. I really don't want to talk about it any longer."

"Hey, would you like a chocolate chip cookie?"

"No, thanks."

"Are you OK? You've never said no to sugar before. Are you on Sugarbusters? Or is Ben motivating you to cut back on sweets?"

She's teasing me? That little ...

"No – please – no. I'm having lunch in just a bit and I won't be eating sugar. Not because I want to lose weight. It's just that excess sugar is not good for you. My body is a sacred temple that needs to be taken care of with lots of TLC. Losing weight is just a side effect of the love I feel for my own body. If we want the best of life, we need to give life our best. And it all starts with us!"

"You made me lose my appetite. Annie, you're really weird."

"Let's get back to reality, Ashley. Enough chitchat. Lunchtime is just around the corner so I need to get ready."

Ashley perks up noticeably. "Get ready for what?"

Duck and cover, Annie Joseph! If Ashley knows you're having lunch with Ben, it will be the top story on CNN tonight.

"Get ready for a holy moment: lunch."

Warning from the Zen Ministry of Mental Health: going to the fairy tale club turns people into New Age hippies. Before you know it, I'll be smudging my cubicle with sage and boring people at cocktail parties with talk of my "Third Eye Chakra."

"Oh-kaaaay. You're definitely weird! Is RSW teaching you these things?"

"Yes, she is!"

"I think RSW is amazing. I wonder what she's like. Do you have any idea? Is she married? Is she rich? I wonder what RSW means? Maybe 'Rich, Sexy Woman'?"

Ashley smiles at her own little joke.

"Ashley, let's do some work."

At the moment, my Internet research has shifted from Cinderella club blogs to dream getaways. I'm checking out Web sites on vacation spots that look like different incarnations of the Garden of Eden while picturing myself playing Eve to Ben's Adam (minus evil snakes and pesky apples, of course). That's what's great about being a journalist: You can relax in front of the computer, travel to exotic locations and still pass it off as "research." In between islands, I head to the bathroom to listen to Ben's message. I lock myself in a stall and proceed to play it over and over smiling like an idiot. OK, just one more time ...

"Hi, Annie, this is Ben ..."

Even with my OCD incident in the rest room, lunchtime takes forever to arrive. As I'm crossing the street to meet Ben, I feel like a teenager again. Like I felt on my first kiss with Alex in his Escort convertible. He was so fine! He looked like Eric Estrada from "CHiPs" only I ate all the chips. OK, bad joke.

I remember that night like it was yesterday. We went to my neighbor's party in her parents' garage. I was feeling so sexy. I had on my favorite perfume; a faux Giorgio of Beverly Hills that I actually got for $5 at a yard sale. Alex wore a red Polo shirt – a real one, not one of the countless '80s knockoffs – with white hightops and a nice-fitting pair of Levi's. I wore a black-and-white striped mini-dress and Revlon Hot Red lipstick. I waited all evening for that kiss, and when the time came, it was indeed unforgettable. Unforgettable because it was the worst kiss I ever had – mushy, pushy and reeking of cigarettes and keg beer. In short, nothing like the kiss between Molly Ringwald and that hunky, brooding guy in "Sixteen Candles."

I left that party hugely disappointed and didn't kiss anyone for years. Oh, fairy godmother, please help me! I can see him across the room, sitting in a corner. I think I'm going to die from spontaneous combustion. My legs have turned to Jell-O. OK, calm down, Annie. After all, it's just lunch. Who knows? He might decide to ignore me while checking out all the cute waitresses. Or maybe he's already heard I'm ga-ga over him and wants to tell me – gently, because he's a nice guy – that we should just be friends. Oh, he's spotted me and is waving. There's no turning back now. Annie Joseph, you need to embrace your dreams and desires. So just picture yourself marrying Ben in a beautiful ceremony and leaving each other love poems on the answering machine.

"Hi, Ben. How're you doing?"

My casualness surprises me.

"Fine. I really wanted to see you again."

"Me too."

(Oops! Mustn't appear too eager.) He is looking at me with a special look in his eyes. I can't tell whether he is really happy to see me again or is he looking at my outfit and thinking to put my picture in his magazine's "Don't" feature. Well I forgot that he works for a men's magazine, and in this particular case, whether it has this kind of thing for sure. "Don't" would be pictures of women's with clothes and "Do" would be naked women. Relax, Annie Joseph. Pretend that you are cool and that just last week you were out four times on a date with handsome men like Ben.

"I had such a great time visiting with you. I just wanted to see you again!"

"I wanted to see you too!"

So much for acting blasé. I wanted to blurt everything to him. Dear Ben, you have no idea how badly I wanted to see you, oh sweet future father of my children.

"I just wanted to give you something. You mentioned in the grocery store about one of your favorite bands. Well, it just so happens that in our last music issue we did a story on U2 and I was invited to their show. So I brought you a copy of the magazine with the story in it."

So he hands me a copy of the magazine. You're kidding me. OK, he gets points for listening to what I said at the store but just a magazine with my favorite band? He doesn't think I work in the same building? He doesn't think the day Bono was in there I staked out the elevators all day to try to catch a glimpse of the man? OK, Cinderella, I will give my best in this moment and focus on the positive.

"Oh, Ben, thanks. That is so thoughtful."

I page through the magazine and in the middle of it is a DVD. I pick it out of the magazine and see it is signed by … Bono!

"It is a copy of the stage cameras that night when they played in town. You said that you were at the show, so I thought you might like it. And, well with Bono's signature…"

Oh, my God! Do I do what I am learning at the Cinderella meetings about following my true desires and jump on this man's lap and tell him how wonderful this is, or do I pretend that yesterday Sting stopped by my cube and helped me with my form on the downward dog? It's better I opt for a more civilized and mature approach.

"No way! You're kidding me?"

I start giggling like a 12-year-old girl. I can't stop. I am so nervous with excitement. This is the most thoughtful gift anyone has given me. I cannot stop laughing. I need to control myself and say something clever to him right now.

"Thank you so much, Bono – I mean Ben. Well, Ben, please tell Bono I say thanks. Not that Bono would care about me or if you're talking to him you would even talk about me."

Oh, fairy godmother, now is the time to use your little wand to shut my mouth or at least make something that makes some sense come out of it ...

"So how are you, Bono? Uhh, I mean Ben. How are you, Ben?

Oh, God, I'm delirious. That's good, Annie, way to dazzle him with this deep and profound question.

"I am fine, Annie, and I am glad you liked it. I will have trouble parting with it, but it sounded like you love the band as much as I do so I knew it at least would be in good hands."

"Good hands? Are you kidding. I don't think I will ever touch it again. This was so thoughtful. Thank you so very much."

"No problem. I wanted to give this DVD to you today because I'm going out of town tomorrow. A business trip. I'll be back on Gabrielle's wedding day. Are you going to the wedding?"

"She invited me, but I'm still not sure I'll be able to make it."

"Maybe we can go together."

"I'm not sure I can go. I'll have to check my calendar; I think I have a commitment that day. I'll see."

Damn! He's going to be out of town for a week? I'm already in pain. What's wrong with me? This is a guy I barely know. A guy I never even kissed, yet he's everything to me. I just want to go to sleep until he returns. I'm sorry, Cinderella, but now I'd do anything to be Sleeping Beauty. I didn't want to go to Gabrielle's wedding, but now I have to go. What about clothes, huh? I can't wear that purple dress again, or he'll think I'm the lost eggplant from the Fruit of the Loom guys. Which reminds me: I haven't shaved my legs since the Clintons were in the White House and I'm hairier than an Italian Teamster. If I want to go from Chevy Impala to Lexus, I have to get some serious bodywork this weekend.

"You're a good friend of Gabrielle's, aren't you?"

"I love Gabrielle. We're really good friends!"

Not to be paranoid, but why is he asking me about Gabrielle? Maybe he's still burning a torch for her, even though she's engaged to a nice investment banker? Damn Uber-Barbie!

Very subtly (I hope), I fish for more information.

"I noticed you seem to be really good friends."

"We have to because we're cousins. I carried her in my arms when she was a little baby. I actually helped her get this job."

Try to resist the urge to turn cartwheels right down the middle of the restaurant, Annie. And put away your .38.

"That's great! Wow, I didn't know you are cousins."

"Yes, we are."

Ben's eyes crinkle adorably as he smiles. We continue to talk and laugh so much that we don't even notice how time flies. Our one-hour lunch stretches to one-and-a-half hours, then two. I start to feel guilty then think of my five years of 15-minute vending machine lunches spent hunched over my keyboard. For once, I figure, Women & Co. owes me a real lunch.

Ben talks about his seemingly idyllic childhood; I talk about mine. I actually find myself babbling about my Carnie Wilson complex – as though I was always the "fat girl" they had to hide behind a bush in the music video. With Ben, I can just be myself. I don't even know who the hell I am, but with him I can be myself. That's the way I feel, even though it doesn't make any sense. I have never unveiled my soul like this on a second date! I don't need to hide anything from him – except my hairy legs.

We don't seem headed for a kiss, even though I want to so badly. As we say our good-byes, he says:

"I hope this week flies so it doesn't feel like I've been away from you long. I'd love to go to the wedding with you. I'll call you when I come back."

And then he kisses me – on my forehead! That's just great. I almost explode from spontaneous combustion, and all I get is a lousy kiss on my forehead. I don't know whether he will be the man who is going to do everything to bring me "passion fruit" but what I know is that for the first time in many years I feel my life is changing and I feel in my heart it's just the beginning.

Chapter 8

What I want From Life? Passion Fruit!

Much *to my surprise, the week goes by quickly. I devote my time, energy and creativity to getting my collection of short stories ready for a meeting with the publisher. I rewrite, review and rewrite some more. The process seems to fill every spare minute, and I can't stop myself from tweaking and retweaking the copy. I wake up early every morning to do more revisions. Truth is, I've decided to put all the teachings into practice so I can write a killer story for the magazine. It's my duty as a journalist. As simple as that.*

To be honest, part of me is still convinced it's a hoax. I don't put all my faith in this Cinderella baloney. Oh sure, I can't deny that my life has improved tremendously, but that's just strange coincidence. My life was going nowhere for so long that it's just logical it would finally take a turn for the better. When Ben leaves a message on my voicemail ("Hi, it's just me. Sorry I missed you!"), it takes all I have not to listen to it 300 times. I really should get tested for OCD. OK, OK, so Cinderella does seem to be influencing me in some bizarre way, even if I still struggle sometimes with seeing her as a heroine. The perfect man, after all, rescued her. And now I'm expecting the same thing! Argh! My inner feminist keeps pestering me. Is this why my generation was raised to be successful and independent – so we could trot off into the sunset with a knight astride his white horse? But right now I am so happy that nothing – not even a personal appearance by Gloria Steinem herself – can sway me. For the first time in years, I feel loved.

The woman I talked to at the publishing house seemed very pleasant and committed to reading the book. At that time, she promised me I would hear from her sometime in the next month. My heart is filled with hope. What if my book gets published? It's what I've always dreamed of! Picture a book signing at a huge bookstore in New York. I'm wearing a gorgeous white suit (I'll be 20 pounds thinner by then) and smiling graciously while signing my adoring fans' books.

But what I'm really happy about this week is getting in touch with Natalie, Liz's daughter. After several long phone conversations, she finally agrees to fly in and meet with her mother next week. Liz deserves it! Knowing how much seeing her daughter would bring her joy helps me realize how valuable random generous acts can be.

All this is going through my mind as I wait at Optimum, the city's trendiest hair salon, drinking herbal tea and having the pedicurist make my nails look like they don't belong on a Spinosaurus. I'm getting all pretty for Gabrielle's wedding. OK, who am I kidding? It's all for Ben. I'm starting to feel like a million bucks; in fact, I think I've spent about that much on the new hairstyle, manicure, facial and pedicure. Let's just hope they don't need to break out the power sander to file down these toenails. As I reach for my cell to check messages, I feel like a pampered doctor's wife. Anyone watching probably assumes I'm checking with the family chef to see whether he's serving salmon or crab tonight. Oh, great! A new message from Ben:

"Hi, this is Ben. I just got back from my trip. I'm one of the ushers, so I guess I'm in charge of taking the bride to the church. I won't be able to go with you, but I'd love to see you at the wedding. I miss your smile. Call me when you have a chance! Bye!"

Hello? The same man who could hook up with any gorgeous supermodel says he misses MY smile? OK, I've lost six pounds since I started the Cinderella Chronicles, but I'm a long way from working the catwalk in Milan. And it sucks that I won't be able to go to the church with him. Still, for him to miss my smile is beyond words. Just for fun, I press the message button again.

"Hi, this is Ben. I just got back from my trip ..."

By the time I return to my apartment, I feel as if I've been through beautification boot camp. All this exfoliating and getting my hair straightened is a full-time job. Actually, taking care of my "outside" for once is kind of fun. For a moment, it's all about YOU. Forget the pipe that burst in your bathroom and flooded your apartment. Forget that you've created an imaginary friend/star reporter who your boss now wants to meet. Right now, the hardest existential question to answer is:

"Iced Mauve or Cherries in the Snow nail polish?" In a half hour, Ashley's going to pick me up to go to the wedding to meet with my Prince Charming. (Only Cinderella could get away with showing up at parties alone.)

I shimmy into my latest purchase: a coral silk wrap dress that flatters my curvy figure – and also happened to be on a fantastic sale. I appraise myself in the mirror, and for once I like what I see. Still, that niggling worry remains: What if our first kiss is as bad as my first kiss with Alex? What if he doesn't like MY kisses? What if he doesn't even try to kiss me? Oh my gawd, what if he's gay? The evidence is overwhelming: He's good-looking, dresses well, sensitive, talks longingly of his mother. He is sooo batting for the other team! OK, Annie Joseph, you really need to chill! Even if Ben turns out to be "Ben Gay," that won't stop you from trying to find your big love, right?

Wrong. Good things happen only to other people. SOS, Cinderella! At this point, my only hope is that Ashley turns into my fairy godmother and transforms the doorman into my Prince Charming.

So I've finally made it. I'm at the reception, listening to "Celebration" by Kool & the Gang. Thankfully, Ashley and her boyfriend were late. I missed all that "in sickness and in health" talk, blah, blah, blah. B-O-R-I-N-G. I'd like to interview Cinderella after 10 years of marriage, when she's hiding her big butt and her cellulite in a big flowery muumuu. And Prince Charming is balding and doesn't even try to hide his beer belly. I'd love to see them after years of tolerating each other, farting and morning breath included. Why am I so bitter? I think my frustration started to build up in the car after witnessing Ashley and her boyfriend's groping and nauseating baby talk.

"You are so purty."

"You're the one who is purty! Does my sweetie love me?"

"Yeah, baby. I adore you!"

I've never felt comfortable at wedding receptions. I think they mess with every woman's self-esteem. Especially that of women over 35. The worst part is seeing people you haven't talked to in years. They never fail to ask the dreaded question: "So, are you married yet?" What motivates people to ask such personal questions? It makes me want to shoot back: "No, I'm not. Are you and Bill still having marital problems?" Or, "Is it true that your hubby cheated on you with a 23-year-old bike messenger? Wow, that must make you feel really old, huh?" Ha! That would show them.

Unfortunately, I haven't talked to Ben at all. Come to think of it, I haven't even seen him. Where on earth could he be? It's hard enough sitting next to Ashley and her creepy boyfriend while listening to Barry Manilow. Why do they always play such tacky music at these things? Ben, my love, where are you? I came to this wedding reception only to see you. I spent half my paycheck on this Donna Karan number only because of you.

Speaking of which, Gabrielle's gown – an exquisite ivory Vera Wang – is perfection. They say all brides are beautiful, but leave it to Gabrielle to look like a walking Vogue cover. I don't know her well, but she seems to be of the high-maintenance variety. Why is it that girls like this always get guys to marry them? And girls like me, who are nice and would never nag their husbands about leaving the toilet seat up, stay single? And where is Ben anyway? I've been tracking him so vigilantly through the crowd – quietly watching as he plays the perfect gentleman and visits with the old ladies or poses with the bridal party for pictures. I've worked so hard not to seem too anxious or needy. Be calm, Annie Joseph. Your time together will come.

Yum, they're serving those tiny bacon and leek quiches. It's a shame saturated fat isn't good for you; I would extend my life by 10 years just by grazing on this buffet. Must remember: I have to give life my best so I can receive the best. I'm not going to become even more neurotic about food. It won't hurt to eat a little bit of something fattening, right? They're so small; three or four can't hurt. Why is this guy videotaping my table just as I'm stuffing my face with appetizers? Heidi Klum may look elegant while scarfing down quiche, but not me, honey! If I don't find Ben within the next five minutes, I'm going to fill my bag with petit fours and teensy meatballs and get out of here.

"Shall we dance?"

Oh, that familiar, beautiful, wonderful voice. My heart magically migrates to my throat.

"Uh, hi, Ben. You startled me! We didn't make it to the church on time. I haven't seen you here at the reception at all."

"I'm so happy you came. I really wanted to dance with you. But you know how these parties are. You have to say hi to people you barely know and will never see again for the rest of your life. This sure is a big crowd. Gabrielle seems to know everyone."

I attempt a hollow laugh.

"Oh, yes, how true."

Oh, gawd, he smells so good and – surprise, surprise – looks unbelievable in a tux. Before I know it, he's leading me out on the crowded dance floor. He may be the only man on earth who can make me happy dancing to "When a Man Loves a Woman." I've always hated that song. But now I love it, right down to Michael Bolton's schmaltzy delivery. Love is like magic. I'm going to download this song to my computer at home so I can remember this moment forever. I wonder whether Cinderella felt like this too when she danced with her prince.

Bolton's crooning ends much too soon, morphing into "Play that Funky Music." As if on cue, 80 percent of the women head for the bathroom. As usual, there is a line outside the stalls. I'm still in my own little world, thinking about our slow dance, when out of the blue a striking, older woman turns to me.

"Are you Annie?"

"Yes, I am."

She extends a hand.

"It's great to meet you. I'm Sonia, Ben's mother. He's been raving about you all day."

Well, lady, wave bye-bye to your beautiful son because I plan to disfigure him with 7,000 kisses tonight. Wake up, Annie! Are you aware that he spoke about you to his mother? That means you're someone special in his life. Or maybe it just means he finds you interesting. I'd better stop thinking about it and start trying to impress the woman for whom I plan to produce 17 grandchildren. I give her my sweetest Girl Scout smile and hope she can't smell the liquor on my breath.

"He raved about you too, especially your cooking. He told me he misses going back home for dinner. He misses seeing you with your apron on cooking his favorite meal."

She grins, and I can see where Ben gets his smile.

"Pasta with basil tomato sauce. Every time he comes to visit I cook it for him."

Even his mom is nice. So nice, in fact, that I now secretly think of her as my mother-in-law-to-be. After our little bonding session in the bathroom, she tells Ben she wants to go home early and is getting another ride home. Then she goes above and beyond the call of MIL duty. She tells Ben he should be a gentleman and take me home. So this is why he's now sitting on my ratty sofa while I desperately rifle through the medicine cabinet, trying to find some mouthwash to help mask the cocktail breath. I really shouldn't have had that fourth Manhattan. If I try to kiss him, he's going to think I'm a drunken slut.

Be strong, Annie Joseph. Go to the living room and just say something. What if everything works out really well? If we start dating, everyone will be gossiping at the office. If we "break up" – as if there's anything to break up from – everyone will be gossiping at the office. It's a lose-lose situation, so I'll just not worry about it and wish myself good luck.

"Did you find your cell?" he asks when I finally emerge from the bathroom.

"No, I lost it at the reception. It's OK. I'll get a new one. I'll go make some coffee."

He grabs my hand and pulls me down on the couch.

"You know, Annie. Even though we've known each other for only a short period of time, you're really special to me. Can I ask you something?"

"Sure. What's that?"

He proceeds to shut my mouth – with the best kiss of my life! Forget about my first kiss and his beer breath; I've never felt like this before! Is he enjoying this as much as I am? Is that humanly possible? He doesn't have a clue that he's the most important man in my life. I want to be with him for the rest of the day, the rest of the week, the rest of my life. Oh, honey, the joy!

Oh, oh, he is slipping his hands between my thighs. He's trying to unbutton my shirt. Do I let him or not? Wait, I already have "let" him! It's so exciting to feel his lips kissing my breasts. He's pulling my skirt up. Oh, no! He's going to think I'm easy. Oh, come on! Who cares! Oh, the kissing, the smell, the passion. I want to give this man my whole being: my body, my heart, my soul – wait. My body and soul?

I can't do this! My body and heart are sacred. I can't give my all to a man I'm not sure would give me passion fruit. I deserve a man who would search the world to bring me passion fruit. How many times have I given my body and soul to a man and never heard from him again? I'd lie to myself with a pep talk: "Well, you're a strong, independent woman. You used him too! I couldn't care less whether he calls me again." But the pain of feeling abandoned and used would never go away, no matter how peppy my self pep talk was!

You know what? I deserve the best. To me, sex is not just about sex anymore. It's about intimacy. I haven't had a chance to be intimate with Ben. The sexual desire is strong, but I can't succumb to it. It's like refusing a Snickers bar: It hurts to say no to the wonderful endorphin buzz of sugar and chocolate. And boy, he offers a better endorphin buzz than most. I want to cry. I think I drank too much. I deserve passion fruit – I want passion fruit.

"Stop … Ben … please, stop!"

He looks startled.

"What's wrong? Why did you push me away like that?"

I'm blurting out words, trying to make sense.

"You didn't do anything wrong. I was doing it to myself. I don't want that for myself. Maybe it would be better if you left."

"Why are you crying? Did I hurt you? Was it that bad?"

"I don't want to say anything. Please, get your stuff and leave. I want to be alone, I want to cry, and I'm really embarrassed to have you see me like this."

"This isn't what you wanted?"

"I need a man who'll drive all over the country to bring me passion fruit. That's what I want from a man. A man who will do anything and everything to make me happy!"

Poor Ben. He looks baffled.

"Passion fruit? Are you OK? I think you've had too much to drink."

"I'm fine, I'm fine. I don't know whether you can understand this, but I met this woman – this nice, wise woman – who had married her soul mate. And do you know how she knew he was the one? She didn't go to Match.com. She didn't meet him at a bar, then Google his name to see whether he already had a family of seven and a record for arson."

Ben is staring at me as if a pink alien just exploded from my stomach. But I can't stop myself. I'm blubbering and boozy now, spouting words between loud, embarrassing sobs.

"Do you know what he did? H-h-he brought her passion fruit. Today, we are all connected by technology and dating services and chat rooms, but we, we're not connecting with our hearts. Our hearts, Ben! Don't you understand?"

Ben slowly shakes his head. His forehead is crumpled in confusion, somehow making him even more beautiful. Great. I look like Courtney Love on a bender – complete with mascara and snot pouring down my face – and he still resembles an artfully confused Adonis.

"Don't you see? People aren't listening to their hearts – th-their intuition! That's what my friend Liz did. When her future husband showed that one simple little act – the act of bringing her passion fruit – she listened to her heart. She knew he wanted to make her happy! He didn't have to have a degree from Harvard or drive a Porsche. He just had to show he would do anything for her because he loved her so much. That's all I want, too. Just one simple act, Ben, to make me happy. I just want a passion fruit."

"I really don't get what you're saying, Annie. You're hungry for passion fruit?"

"No, no!"

I'm frustrated at my own babbling and his failure to comprehend.

"Please, just leave. This isn't what I want at all."

Ben's face darkens with a look – is it anger? – and he pops up off the couch.

"I don't know what you're talking about it, but it's obvious you don't want me here."

He pulls on his tux jacket.

"If I'm not the man you want and I upset you this much and you want me to leave, there's nothing I can do about it."

I just stand there, as if caught in a bad dream. Why don't I say something? Why don't I stop him?

"I'm sorry if I offended you. Take care!"

And just like that, he's gone.

Take care? When a man says this to you, he might as well say "Lady, don't sit by the phone because you'll never hear from me again." And that's exactly what happened. Five days after the Night From Hell – an event I've glumly dubbed "The Passion Fruit Incident" – I'm sullenly reading the Women & Co. Web site at my desk. Judging by the rapturous comments sent by readers, the magazine has a new star: RSW. This does nothing to assuage my depression.

After The Passion Fruit Incident, I spent the whole Sunday nursing a horrible hangover, crying my eyes out and wondering how long I could live off welfare if I quit my job. Since I started going to association meetings, many things have happened: the RSW story, Cathy's eye-opening advice, an attempt to recapture long-forgotten dreams, the realization I miss my dad, a quick unfinished fling with Ben. I need time to get my thoughts in order. I considered calling Ben, but I didn't have the courage to do it. He's not calling me because he probably thinks I'm certifiably insane. He's probably already in the arms of some woman who doesn't drink too much, turn down his advances and then babble senselessly about tropical fruit. I'm too depressed to even flip open my new cell phone.

It's a good thing I lost the other one because I'd wanted to switch providers anyway. Yes, that's the only thing I have to look forward to nowadays – figuring out a new cell phone that never rings. With my luck, if it did ring, it would be some pervert who accidentally misdialed the number for "900-BUSTY BABES." Man, I am so pathetic. When a journalist can't open her cell, it means she needs Prozac injected straight into her veins – or maybe she just needs a man. A man exactly like Ben.

A familiar voice jostles me into the present.

"Annie, wake up! You look so tired this week. Did you have a good time at the wedding reception? How about you and Ben? You haven't said anything about him. I've noticed you two haven't talked at all this week. He's such a hunk! Are you guys dating?"

I turn to Ashley and fix her with a long, somber glare. Then, slowly and purposefully – as if I'm explaining to a preschooler how to detonate a bomb – I set her straight.

"Listen, Ashley, I need to ask you a favor. If you have any kind of compassion toward humanity, then please don't tell me anything about him, don't ask me about him and don't even mention his name to me."

It's better to make this clear to her now, before she starts spreading rumors about us around the office. Then she's going to gossip about who his latest love interest is. And I don't want to hear about him being with another woman – ever. It's way too painful.

"Uh, OK. Sorry Annie. Say, did you tell Liz her daughter is coming to visit next week?"

"I don't want to tell her anything yet. I'm going to bring Natalie to her house. I want it to be a surprise. I don't want her to be hopeful and then her daughter changes her mind at the last minute. Family affairs are very delicate. Anything can happen."

"I'm so interested in this Liz story. Could you tell me more about it? Do you think it could turn into a cover story? If so, could you mention my role in digging up Natalie? That would really impress Paige. It might be just what I need to get a full-time job here."

Not in the mood to help out insufferable interns, I sigh.

"Listen, I'm not in the mood to talk about it right now, but I'll fill you in sometime, OK? And I'm really not doing the Liz thing for a story. I just want to help her out because she's such a nice lady."

The last few weeks of my life were like a Technicolor fairy tale. This week everything's gone back to dreary black and white. I actually miss Liz and the other people at the seminars. So much has happened in the last month. Amazing how quickly the bottom can drop out of your world. I'd forgotten how great it is to be in love until I met Ben. Should I call him? After all, I was the one who told him to get the hell out of my house. But why didn't he call me? Maybe he just wanted a one-night stand. That's not what I want anymore. It's not the best choice for me. I refuse to get anything but the best from life.

It hurts and saddens me, but not all is lost: The publisher's e-mail arrived. So soon? This has to be good news. It looks as if I'm going to be a published writer! Maybe it actually was worth it to follow my dreams. I have to thank Cinderella. I haven't found my Prince Charming yet, but I'll fulfill my biggest dream: to be a "real" writer.

I click on the e-mail to open it. "Thank you for your interest in our company," it reads. "We like your work. However, this is not the type of book we're looking for."

"This type of book?" Why don't you just say "This junk you call a book?" Are you happy now, Cinderella? I worked day

and night to get this book published. And what do I get? A big, fat NO at one of the low points in my life! Unlike you, Cinderella, I didn't have a fairy godmother who could make my dreams come true. Are you happy, you stupid little ninth-century princess and all you crazy cult followers? You watch me publish an article about you, missy! Nobody will want to go to these meetings after the press I give them. The only possible reason I'll go to association meetings is because of dear Liz and to subject this crazy organization to the ultimate hatchet job.

And to think I almost fell for all that baloney about becoming a heroine! The only thing I got out of all this is losing six pounds. But when I get home, I'm going to gain them all back after eating 16 pounds of chocolate in one sitting. I'm crushed! Back to square one. Back to the place I never really left. My testimonial will read: "After meeting Cinderella, my life made a 360-degree turn."

I'm getting out of here. I'm going to make up an excuse, go to that new gourmet candy shop that opened on Quaker Street, eat like a pig and then get ready to uncover this Cinderella quackery for once and for all.

"Annie! Why are you leaving so early? Paige wants to talk to you – something about RSW."

If Ashley calls me "Annie" with that saccharine-sweet tone one more time, I'm going to whack her. And why can't Paige just e-mail me like anyone else? Probably because it's so much more queen-like to summon me with her Royal Bitch Phone.

"I've got an assignment. Just tell her that I left before you had a chance to talk to me."

"Can't you just drop by her office for a couple of minutes? She did say it was urgent."

I dig my keys out of my purse. What are they stuck on?

"Can't right now. It will just have to wait till tomorrow."

What's so urgent anyway? That everyone loves RSW? Have they found out that RSW is a Really Stupid Woman? I can't wait for this nightmare to end.

Chapter 9

Boys Don't Cry ... Heroes Do

After *pigging out on undisclosed quantities of Belgian chocolate, I wipe the evidence off my mouth and head to the association's meeting. I don't charge into the room hurling expletives at Cinderella only because I bump into Liz on my way in. She fixes me with a warm smile.*

"Hi, Annie! I've missed you. Say, I hate to bug you about this, but did your journalist friends find out anything about my daughter? I'm so nervous I haven't been able to sleep."

I work at being evasive – a skill I've perfected since getting caught up in this fairy tale fiasco.

"I can't promise anything but you never know. You might hear of a development this week."

Liz's face lights up.

"What did your friends say?"

"Oh, nothing. It's just that they're so good they might find your daughter sooner than we think."

Her eyes brim with tears.

"You can't imagine how wonderful that would be. I can't wait to be able to hug my daughter again. I hope she forgives me for disappointing her and not being there when she needed me the most."

I want to reach out and give Liz a hug, but my heart hardens at her display of childish optimism. Surely, she wouldn't be setting herself up for such a hard fall if it weren't for people like Cathy and the association.

"It's very hard to forgive, Liz. It's hard to forget the ugly things people have done to us and how much they've hurt us. Maybe that's why your daughter hasn't tried to contact you before."

"I don't want her to forget what happened. I know it's not easy. To me, forgiving is not about forgetting the old story. It's about giving a chance to write a new story."

"Please, don't raise your hopes too much, Liz. We're not sure whether they found her."

I can't give her any reassurance. What if Natalie refuses to see her mother and breaks her poor heart? I pray Natalie will decide to show up. I would give anything to see Liz's face when she saw her daughter again. I know that would make her so happy, and she really is so deserving of happiness. What she said was just beautiful: "Forgiving is not about forgetting the old story. It's about giving a chance to write a new story." I had never thought of it that way.

Forever the mother, Liz quickly switches the attention away from herself.

"Honey, your eyes don't have that special sparkle anymore. What happened? Is it about the young man?"

I attempt a weak smile.

"Yes, it's the young man. I realized he's not the man for me. As soon as I told him I wanted someone to bring me passion fruit, he vanished into thin air."

She laughs.

"Did you really tell him about the passion fruit?"

"I did."

"Sweetheart, young men from the city don't understand the way we old folks used to express ourselves in the country. Don't get depressed. Relationships are like an apple tree: You plant the seed, watch it grow and eventually you'll reap fruit. Today, in our fast-food culture, people are always in a hurry. One month ago, you were madly in love with him. Today you've already given up on him. Human beings are not Hot Pockets that can satisfy your hunger in two-and-one-half minutes. Each person takes time to mature. Take it easy. If he's meant to be your man, then he will be. A rose seed that was planted will grow to be a rose, even though it looks like a bean sprout."

I laugh despite myself.

"You and your gardening metaphors, Liz. You can make me laugh even when I'm going through an emotional storm."

"As long as you're alive, you'll have storms in your life. Imagine if there was no rain, only sunshine. Then plants would die of thirst. Rain is needed to water the plants. It's the same with your life – it needs storms to grow."

I smile at another gardening reference. She can't help herself – but she still makes a lot of sense.

"Thanks Liz. I needed to hear that."

"Oh, hurry; let's get a seat! Cathy looks like she's ready to start."

I feel a maddening combination of anger and sadness. For a few brief periods of time, I really thought I had found the secret to living a full life. And look at me now: still the same! No, wait – it's worse. Before Cinderella, I had no hope and therefore no disappointment. After Cinderella, I believed I could meet the love of my life, work to fulfill my dreams, give people the best of me and be generous – only to discover I really was kidding myself. I didn't even get a lousy T-shirt. Ha! What has Lady Cinderella to say about all this? I'm ready for a showdown.

Cathy is as chipper as ever.

"Good evening. Today we're going to talk about a vital passage in Cinderella's story, a passage that can be part of the story of any hero or heroine. The moment in which, while the hero is giving it his best, his world falls apart and his dreams look as if they're not going to be fulfilled. Let us read this passage:

" 'Determined, Cinderella finished all her work, helped her stepsisters get dressed and found one of her stepmother's gowns in a trunk. With the small animals' help, she used remnants of her stepsisters' dresses to create her dress and then got ready.

" 'When Cinderella's stepsisters saw her, they recognized the fabrics of their own gowns so they tore up the dress and left for the palace screaming with laughter. Cinderella lost all hope and was so sad that she started to cry.' "

And Cathy continues with a gentle tone in her voice:

"All of a sudden you're sad; you lose hope. That dream you worked so hard on falls apart right in front of you. That relationship you invested so much in is over. That dream you were absolutely sure you were going to fulfill didn't come true. That person you thought was going to help you bailed out on you. So like Cinderella, you feel that all your efforts and dreams are torn up, just like the gown that our heroine invested so much time and creativity in. What should we do during these hard times?"

Oh, the silence. I see I'm not the only one whose hopes were shattered.

"There are times in a hero's life when his dreams and hopes are shattered. Sometimes you feel as if you're at a loss and you lack the strength to carry on. You feel as if everything you've done has been in vain. But a heroic life is not just about victories, it's also about overcoming defeats."

Steve's first to speak. No surprises there.

"What do you mean overcoming defeats? A defeat is a defeat. It's over and we lost. It's not something we wonder about."

If Miss Cinderella gives me believable insight into my defeats, I may write an article that's marginally less scathing.

"Steve, in life we go through many difficult situations that we consider defeats. In this part of Cinderella's story, it's obvious that she burst out crying and lost hope. She devoted herself to the ball and all of a sudden her only dress, her only hope, is torn to shreds right in front of her eyes. She didn't know what would happen after her hope was lost. She had no idea she would end up going to the ball in a gorgeous gown. When we forget that the *Grand Life* encourages and strengthens us to fulfill our dreams, we get depressed. Sometimes things don't turn out the way we planned them. They turn out to be much better."

Beatrice, who is now seated beside Steve, stands.

"If this *Grand Life* has everything planned out for us, we just have to sit back and wait for things to happen, right? I mean, why work?"

"Well Beatrice, that's why I spoke in our last meeting, about how important it is to work to fulfill our dreams and always give our best. All I can do is trust that the *Grand Life* is planning something better for me. But it's not going to happen if I don't do my part. Like I said before, the fact that you work hard to fulfill your dreams doesn't mean they will happen the way you want. Don't focus in the results, focus in giving your best. Sometimes if what you had in mind doesn't happen, something better will. If you offer the best to life, you'll get life's best in return. It's the law of physics, the law of action and reaction."

I can't stand it any longer. I have to ask! My head is about to explode. I'm already here so who knows? Maybe Miss Cinderella can help ease my pain, even if it's just by sharing another bumper sticker slogan with me.

"What should we do then during hard times?"

Cathy smiles kindly, as if she understands. It's almost as if she has a crystal ball that showed her my previous week, in all its ugly torment.

"Annie, these are the moments when heroes and heroines are tested. When everything we thought would happen doesn't, we leave our winning hero asleep and our most defeatist thoughts wake up. We tell ourselves, 'Life has no meaning anymore. Nothing is going the way I planned it. I have to quit because I'm just not able to succeed. Everything is going against me in life.' If we start listening to these negative thoughts, then we stop walking side by side with the *Grand Life* toward the fulfillment of our dreams. We choose to listen to the stepsisters laughing at Cinderella instead of ignoring them and staying focused on our dream. That's why during these times, we feel that our strength shrinks and we're headed toward destruction."

I'm not about to sit down.

"You still haven't answered my question: What does one do during difficult times? Cinderella had negative thoughts and her fairy godmother appeared and solved everything with a touch from her magic wand. For those of us who lack a fairy godmother, what can we do?"

Don't even think of giving me a dirty look, Miss Thing, or I'm going to snap your head off like I did with the skinny kids' dolls, back when I was an innocent and sweet child.

"Cinderella cried when she felt hope slipping away from her. But she never complained, cursed or insulted her stepmother and stepsisters. She just cried and allowed herself to feel disappointment. She didn't stop being a heroine because she cried and felt abandoned. When Jesus Christ was on the cross, he cried and said: "My God, my God, why hast thou forsaken me?" A hero has the right to cry. The fact that a hero cries doesn't mean he's weak. Why? Because it takes strength to accept our weaknesses."

I can see Steve, like me, is not satisfied with Cathy's answer. He speaks up.

"So what should we do during these times, Cathy? Watch soap operas, eat Twinkies and sob uncontrollably?"

"Steve, these are the times in which the hero or heroine is most vulnerable."

"What are they vulnerable to?"

"They're vulnerable to what I call their "inner step-mother" – to listen to her defeatist thoughts and thus go in the *Grand Life's* opposite direction. If we don't watch it, we're vulnerable to everyone. To co-workers who say: "Didn't I tell you you're doing it all wrong?" To our closest loved ones saying: "You're never going to get anywhere with that attitude." To the media saying: "The economy is not getting better so why waste time or energy investing your money."

I am frustrated, and a quick scan of my fellow classmates reveals I am not alone. What's this? Dissent in the ranks? I close my eyes and fantasize that the class members are yelling "Mutiny!" as they force Cathy and Cinderella to walk the plank.

"My question is what should we do during these times?"

Beatrice too now, sounding frustrated.

"Could you please just answer that for us?"

"Beatrice, when we find ourselves in difficult situations, we have to put into practice our 'basic hero attitude,' which can incite real transformations in our life. After doing our best, after offering our best, we need to trust that the best will happen to us. And when I say 'the best,' I don't mean what we *want* to happen, rather what needs to happen so each of us can find our true path."

"Talk is cheap. It's not easy to trust when we doubt."

Oh, Steve-o, you said it.

"A hero's journey is not easy, but it's very interesting. It's not for everyone. Not everyone can embark on that journey. We don't choose our circumstances or what happens to us. However, we can choose the way we deal with these circumstances. Your homework for the next couple of weeks is to empower yourselves to deal with your circumstances, with whatever happens in your life, in a positive way. When in the face of negative circumstances we entertain negative thoughts, we increase the odds of achieving negative results."

Steve fires back.

"But Cinderella lost her faith. That's not 'positive.' "

"I'm sure Cinderella did lose hope. She probably felt all the work she'd done to fulfill her dreams had been in vain. All of us have experienced this at one time in our lives. However, right when Cinderella was totally discouraged, she was challenged to put her faith to work in its purest form: trust! Hard times are just a great opportunity for us to put our faith into practice. We need to trust, not only in our own strength but also in the *Grand Life's* strength pushing us toward victory – like a child who, when he throws himself into his father's arms, has complete faith that his father will catch him. He knows his father would never drop him. I think it's important to avoid associating the word "faith" with religion. The faith I'm referring to is the trust and the confidence that when we offer our best to the world, the world will give us its best and thus the best will happen to us. When we have this kind of faith, we attract miracles in our life, we attract the godmother magic."

Even my sweet Liz is questioning now.

"Cathy, you mentioned that during these moments we're vulnerable and may give up our dreams by listening to our 'stepmother.' How can we deal with these pessimistic voices? And how can we have faith during these hard times?"

I thought I would hate this meeting, but it's turning out to be fun. My internal stepmother talked me into defeat. My consolation prize: eating enough candy to gain 20 pounds in 24 hours. I'm sorry I did it. Sorry, poor, overworked pancreas.

"I'm so glad you asked that question, Liz. I'll try to give you a simple explanation because, like I said before, I don't think I have the absolute truth in my hands. Tell me, Liz: Is it easier for a thief to rob your house when you're in the house or away on a trip for a week?"

"When I'm away on a trip."

"The same thing happens with the negative voices. They have power over us only when we're not home."

"I'm not sure I understand what you mean."

"Where are we at this very moment? We're in this room, right? What are we doing? We're paying attention to what's going on in the meeting. When we travel into the past or the future, we leave room for the negative thoughts to come pester us. We allow the stepmother in. And she'll say anything to steal our strength, our faith, our dreams."

"I don't understand, Cathy."

I love Liz's straightforward, unpretentious approach. She's not worried what anyone in the room thinks of her; she just wants to understand. I'm going to miss her when these meetings are over. I can't believe there's just one more to go.

"When we lose hope, we get discouraged because we had decided that something should happen in the *future*, and that something never happened. Cinderella lost hope because she had decided she was going to go to the ball in her mother's gown. But the gown was torn. We also get disappointed when we're bound to our *past* experiences. How many people give up finding their true love because they're still bound to disappointments of the past?"

Er … that would be me.

"When we try to control the *future* or are too bound to the past, we make ourselves vulnerable to those voices and allow them to steal our strength. The only way we can succeed in keeping our strength is by living in the present. We usually allow the voices to influence: 'Cinderella, you can go to the ball only after you finish all your chores.' Cinderella always cleaned the house without showing discontent. However, when she did a chore thinking about what she'd win in the future, she ran the risk of having her present moment stolen by the promise of a future. All of a sudden, we start listening to things like: 'Buy this now, you'll need it in the future.' Or: 'Don't do this so that won't happen in the future.' Or: 'Watch out! Remember what happened last time you did that'?

"These voices generate concern, fear, worry; they basically steal our strength. As soon as you start hearing these voices, embrace the present. Don't think about how you should be somewhere else, having another type of experience, hanging out with other people sometime in the future. You might cry and feel neglected. Just use this time to grow and be stronger. If there's no one around, go ahead and say out loud: 'Because I did my best, I will receive the best.' "

What an eye-opener. Those voices really did a number on me. I was so busy obsessing about the men who had hurt me in the past that I sabotaged my present moment with Ben.

"So this week, learn how to trust in the *Grand Life*. Make sure you're doing your best and trust that the best will happen to you. The best for both your growth and fulfillment. When we have certainty that the best will happen during uncertain moments, we open the door for miracles to happen."

Class time is running out, but Steve's determination is not.

"Wait a minute! Are you saying miracles happen when we trust in the *Grand Life*? Don't you think that's pushing it? To talk about miracles happening in today's world is inconsistent, don't you think?"

"First of all, let me explain what I call a *miracle*. In the dictionary, one of the definitions of miracle is *an extraordinary fact, an incomprehensible, excellent outcome*. In Cinderella's story, the fairy godmother's magic is like a miracle, something incomprehensible by rational thinking. When we hear about miracles, we get the impression that miracles happen for no reason at all. What I am trying to say is that miracles happen because of faith. Faith is responsible for the amazing events in our lives."

"Are you saying that faith generates miracles? Faith in what? Are you a spokesman for the 700 Club?"

"As I've already said, have trust in the *Grand Life*; trust in the strength that encourages us to grow. Trust that when we offer our best, we are going to yield the best."

"Oh come on, Cathy! Surely you acknowledge it's not easy to have faith when we're going through difficult, uncertain times."

"Steve, those are the times when you most need to have faith. Trust me: When we practice faith during our darkest moments, that's when we set in motion the power that turns on the light."

A new voice pipes up from the back of the room.

"The light? I'm confused. What do you mean?"

"Let me give you an example, Judy. When Moses faced the Red Sea, he faced a huge challenge that truly tested his faith. How many people would have thought: "Forget it, we can't go on; we're all going to drown'? Moses kept walking. He set his faith in motion and just trusted, not in his own strength, but in the *Grand Life*. And we know that the *Grand Life* parted the Red Sea. In my personal opinion, this is a symbol of how faith can open new and fantastic roads in our journey toward fulfilling our dreams."

"But you even acknowledged that Cinderella herself lost her faith."

"Steve, when Cinderella began to weep, she realized her own strength was not enough to fulfill her dream. When we surrender and trust in the *Grand Life*, that's when we do our best. When we infuse trust into our doubts and into our indecision, that's when we can produce true miracles. Jesus said: 'Because verily I say unto you, if you have faith as a grain of mustard seed, you will say unto this mountain: transport yourself from here to there, and it will transport itself, and nothing will be impossible for you.' "

This woman never gives up. She really is something else. I think I might even miss her when these classes are over. But come on, this sounds more and more like a religious cult.

"I'm sorry, but I just can't buy into all this bull. It's just too irrational for me. And the fact that you use Biblical examples bugs me. I'm sure many people in here aren't even Christian."

"Steve, why is it that you don't believe you deserve miracles, extraordinary facts in your life? Why don't you empower yourself?"

"Me? Well, I …"

"You don't need to answer. The majority of us were trained to value only the observable and tangible. Talking about miracles sounds like science fiction, doesn't it? I'm not even going to try to convince you to believe in miracles. We know that now even scientists and doctors research the effect of faith in treating diseases. But that's not what I want to talk about. What I'd like you to do is to live with trust and faith in the best, even when you're going through hard times. I also want you to watch the effect this practice has in your life. The only reason I mentioned the Bible passage is because I believe it has a lot to do with what we're talking about. We're not going to ask whether it happened. Everyone has his or her own beliefs. However, we can't deny that a person who has strong beliefs in a new venture, a relationship or a mission is capable of moving mountains that would otherwise keep them from fulfilling their dreams. There are mountains of laziness, of fear, of selfishness, of pride, of prejudice, of discouragement. Faith gives us perseverance, energy and strength to overcome the obstacles. It's obvious that a person with a strong faith can achieve a fantastic life."

Steve is obviously too exhausted to keep debating, so Beatrice jumps in.

"It's confusing to me when you talk about miracles. I never had anything extraordinary happen in my life. What I'm trying to say is, I don't have faith. But I do believe there is a Superior Force that doesn't like me too much."

"Beatrice, it all depends on what you bear in mind when you refer to the occurrence of an extraordinary event. Let me tell you a story. A father is in a hurry because he's late for his business meeting. His son is crying because he can't get his ball. So he asks his dad to get it for him. His father is thinking only about getting to the meeting on time, so he tells his son to ask his mother to get the ball for him. He leaves for work and crashes his car a couple of blocks away from his house. He's severely injured, so they take him to the hospital. The only doctor who could perform his delicate operation has just left. They call him on his cell, but nobody can reach him. All of sudden, out of the blue, almost magically, the doctor comes in. He forgot his cell at the hospital. The surgery is successful and the father goes back to his normal life a couple of months later. Do you believe that's a miracle, an extraordinary event?"

"Well, I guess in some ways it is."

"So, let's play around with the story and change it a little. Suppose that the father, in spite of being in a hurry, takes the time to grab the ball and give it to his crying son. He takes the time to play with his son until the little boy feels better. He gives his son a big hug before he leaves for work. Because of his decision to "waste" five minutes, he avoids the accident. So he continues, peacefully unaware of what he's avoided, through his day. For some people, it's just another day, with no miracles. But for those who have faith, it's an extra day to experience newer and greater miracles!"

"But we are unable to picture that kind of miracle. Like the one in the story."

"That's absolutely true, Beatrice. We're unable to picture this miracle. On the other hand, there are other miracles that are more obvious. Like the one of the mother whose husband left her and she still manages to support her children by overcoming her fear and insecurity. Or the young drug addict who overcomes addiction. Or even that of the businessman who focuses on providing jobs and prosperity to people in lieu of his own profit and gain. A miracle is your being here today, learning how to practice trust and allowing yourselves to overcome the obstacles of insecurity. Life is a great miracle, and this becomes more evident when we empower ourselves to trust.

"This week I want you to empower yourselves to trust, to practice faith. Trust that when we give our best, the best will happen to us. And remember the 'best' is not always what we *want*, but what we *need* to fulfill our dreams. So these next weeks I want you to trust – if you feel sad, trust that this feeling will make you grow toward your happiness. If you are worried, trust that the best will happen. If you don't know what to do, trust the answer will come. Trust! We often have the feeling that our life is far from being a fairy tale, but I believe that by doing our best and practicing faith, we all can achieve happy endings. Have a good week!"

What is the "best" that can happen to me? Ben has disappeared from the face of the earth, and my dream of publishing a book has gone down the drain. I don't have either the heart to look for another publisher or the motivation to work. Only a miracle can save me. But I need to trust that something better is ahead. I'm going to put into practice this business of trust – mainly because there's only one more meeting and I need to write a report about the experience. However, all I want to practice now is going home, putting my head on a pillow and crying my eyes out.

I want to cry because I feel lonely.

I want to cry because I'm afraid.

I want to cry because I feel abandoned.

I want to cry because I'm strong enough to face my weaknesses.

I want to cry because … heroes and heroines cry!

Chapter 10

Help Me!

I drive home feeling as though vultures are circling my head. Actually, more like Cinderella's wicked stepmother and stepsisters, who lean into my ear and cackle: "Your life will never get better. Everything you learned in those meetings won't do a thing for you. You're going to end up an old, angry, lonely woman with arthritis, osteoporosis and bunions so big you'll have to wear shoeboxes on your feet!"

Now I understand why Cathy said dwelling on the future can open the door to those voices whose mission is to upset us. I need to wake up, have faith and trust that only the best will happen to me. There's only one more meeting left. If I get zero results after practicing all this Cinderella stuff, I can always get revenge. I'll just write an article trashing sweet, perfect Cinderella. Oh, "Grand Life," make me strong! I'd better finish RSW's article before I go to bed...

FROM TODAY ON I EMPOWER MYSELF TO CHOOSE:
... COURAGE, INSTEAD OF FEAR.
... FAITH, INSTEAD OF DOUBT.
... LOVE, INSTEAD OF LONELINESS.
... LIGHT, INSTEAD OF DARKNESS.
... ME, INSTEAD OF OTHERS.
... THE OTHERS
... WHO LIVE
... IN ME.

Before leaving for work the next day, I read RSW's article. And you know what? It actually helps me feel better. My eyes were puffy from my latest marathon crying jag, and now they've almost returned to normal. I've been crying more than the lead in a soap opera lately. How can those actresses wail for 90 percent of the show without once smearing their mascara?

I had originally planned to go to work sporting a baggy black outfit and a long face. Instead, thanks to RSW, I decide to wear a nice suit with a fuchsia scarf, high heels and makeup. All I need to do is trust that the best will happen to me today. I choose to trust. After all, I've done my work. I took a risk, submitted my book and the publisher thought it was a piece of junk. Who knows, maybe something better is around the corner. As far as Ben is concerned; well, there's no denying I miss him. Maybe I should call him. Maybe I shouldn't. He probably thinks I'm a deranged passion fruit addict. Is that why he hasn't called me? I know I messed up but still. He's probably forgotten about me by now. Anyway, enough obsessing already! I must have faith that the best will happen – even though I'm about to be assaulted by Ashley and that voice. That voice would have turned Gandhi into a homicidal maniac.

Once again, Ashley is playing my personal warden. You'd never guess she's a good 10 years younger than me.

"Annie! You must go to Paige's office ASAP. She's been wanting to talk to you since yesterday. I think it's something to do with RSW. I wonder what it's about. Did they find out where she's hiding?"

And once again, my attempts to be tolerant and kind belly-flop.

"It looks to me as if you have nothing better to do than meddle in other people's lives, Ashley. Don't you have any real work to do? Does gossip drive your life? Perhaps you were inspired to study journalism while reading *The National Enquirer* during a pedicure?"

There's just one meeting left, Annie Joseph. Be nice to Ashley. Remember, give your best to the world and trust that you will receive the best in return. It's not about magic and the fairy godmother; it's about physics and the law of action and reaction.

"Sorry Ashley, you didn't deserve that."

It's worth it for her smile.

"When is Liz's daughter visiting her?"

"Natalie said she'd be flying in tomorrow evening."

"Ooh, tomorrow? Can I go with you?"

"Absolutely not. I want you to do me a favor. Here is Liz's full name. I met her through the association. Track down her phone number and address for me."

"No problem. The association? What association? Oh, I get it! You and Liz are AA members."

Boy, she sure picked the wrong time to play dumb. As if she doesn't know what "the association" is by now. I've only been talking about it for weeks.

"No, Ashley, I'm not an AA member. But I may be a platinum card-carrying member of Tormented Cubicle-mates Anonymous."

"Is that supposed to be funny?"

I poke my tongue out at her as I rush out of our cubicle for my meeting with Paige.

I wonder what's so urgent. Did it finally happen? Did she find out that RSW is me? Oh, there I go again. Thinking about the future instead of focusing on the now. I'm inviting my own, private stepmother to ride her broom into my world and harass me with her mind games. As I walk toward Paige's office, I focus on staying in the moment. I'll relax and take in the details: the boring beige carpet, the banged-up metal desks, Paige's bimbo assistant trying to pretend she isn't on the phone with her boyfriend.

I put on my brightest face and stride confidently into Paige's office.

"Hi, Paige! You wanted to speak to me?"

Resplendent in a sapphire suit, Paige looks up from a hodgepodge of magazines, all flipped open to RSW's latest column.

"I tried to talk with you yesterday but you had already left. We have some news that I need you to pass along to RSW."

Uh-oh.

"News? What news?"

Don't create stories in your head. Focus on the present. Listen to Paige.

"Are you aware of RSW's success?"

Paige taps pointedly on her leather-covered desk.

"We're talking fabulous potential, perhaps on an international level. There are groups of people studying her articles across the country. There are actual Internet chat rooms devoted to her work."

My stomach feels like one big knot.

"But the articles are so simple. There's nothing special about them."

"As I've said from the beginning, it's that simplicity that seems to touch people."

Paige sounds impatient at my failure to grasp RSW's genius. She's probably wondering how one magazine could employ someone as brilliant as RSW and as clueless as me. If only she knew.

"So what's the big news?"

"Well, I'd rather tell her in person. But I'm guessing that's not possible, right?"

"I'm sorry, Paige, but it isn't. Not right now, anyway. She's really dealing with a lot of anxiety right now."

Annie, you must stop this insanity. Stop lying, girlfriend! If you get caught, your career will never recover. You'll be forever known as the Former Food Hack Who Tried to Lie Her Way to a Better Career. But I didn't want to lie. Oh, God, what to do? Oh, fairy godmother, please get me out of this mess and I'll never ask for anything again."

"Well, of course I understand, but we will have to meet sometime. After all, we've got big plans for your friend. For now, could you please give RSW a message? It's very, very important. One of the country's biggest publishers wants her to publish a book."

"A book? What do you mean?"

In my efforts to think my way out of this mess, I've resorted to repeating everything Paige says. It's better known as "stalling."

"They'd like to publish a compilation of her columns."

Paige taps her vintage Mont Blanc fountain pen on the desktop with excitement.

"It's something that's never been tackled by a *Women & Co.* columnist before. A complete set of self-help articles – everything our readers need to know about living a happy, complete life – under one cover. Of course, what she's written for us so far isn't nearly enough to fill a book. Do you know whether she's written other columns that haven't been published yet? She seems to generate copy fairly quickly. Maybe she could sit down and bang out a bunch of them for us?"

I'm so caught up in the excitement that I'm not thinking straight. A chance to publish a book?

"Uhhh, I guess RSW once told me she loves writing short stories. She has a bunch of stories that she put away in her closet."

Paige sits up even straighter, emphasizing her ballerina posture.

"She already has stories? A collection of short stories by our very own RSW? That's fantastic! The publisher wants to sign a contract as soon as humanly possible. He wants to ride the wave of her popularity before it dies down."

Granted, my exposure to Paige has been relatively limited, but I've never seen her so excited. She is leaning forward in her leather chair now and her pen is tapping like a Tommy Lee drum solo. Ta-da-dum. Ta-da-dum. Ta-da-dum-dum-DUM.

"But we really must hurry. I have just two weeks – an impossible deadline, really – to take care of all the details. They want to introduce her book at the next national book fair. But I can't stress this one point enough: She absolutely has to be there for the book signing. People will be clamoring to meet her. She has to get over this agoraphobia thing if she wants to succeed. Can't she take a Xanax or something?"

Paige is speaking so quickly that I don't have time to reply.

"Oh, and we also have to meet with the publisher right away so we can work out a good deal for her. Do you think RSW will agree to fly to LA in a couple of weeks to review and sign a contract with the publisher? Does she have an attorney?"

"Um, I, I don't know. But I'm sure she'll be interested. Writing is her true calling, her dream!"

What in holy hell am I doing? Do I plan to dress in a hooded death robe to disguise my identity at the book signing?

"How do you know that?"

Paige raises one perfectly shaped eyebrow.

"Well, she always instant messages me. She keeps saying how she wished someone would publish her short stories. Do you think the publisher really will go for this kind of book?"

"Annie, RSW is such a hot commodity right now that he would probably publish a cookbook with RSW's name on it!"

Really? I've got a ton of cheesecake recipes. I manage not to giggle.

"I'll talk to RSW. I mean, I'll write to her. I'll let you know what she says."

Paige has already turned away to type furiously on her Mac.

"By the way, how's your project going? Are you finished with the whole thing?"

"Yeah, almost. One more meeting to go."

"Can't wait to read it."

"Umm, I know what you mean. Talk to you later."

"Ciao. And send my love to RSW."

Holy mess! I'm obviously beyond salvation. OK, fairy godmother, there's nothing you can do for me at this point. Save your magic wand for when am in the unemployment line. My feelings are all over the board: I'm thrilled that my book will get published, and I'm terrified that my lie will be uncovered. Did all this happen because I practiced faith? But wait, Paige already wanted to talk to me yesterday. Maybe I attracted the opportunity with my "heroic attitude." Or maybe it's just an opportunity for public humiliation. Regardless, I worked hard to get this book written and published. I offered the best of myself to the world, and the world – hopefully – offered its best to me. Some people may see it as "luck," but I know the effort I made to have this opportunity.

Hmmm, that's interesting. Things are starting to make sense. But how can I make RSW appear? This will take more than faith; it will take an act of God. If they only knew that RSW stands for Really Stupid Woman. I wonder if I can claim RSW was abducted by aliens? Or maybe she flipped out and is in a psych ward? But then I'll lose the chance to launch her – I mean, MY book. I'll lose the opportunity of a lifetime and the chance to finally fulfill my dreams. Think, Annie, think! What if I tell them I'm a medium and RSW is actually my spirit guide? Who would believe that? No one, probably. I'd have to resort to running a stand on the street with a handmade sign that reads "Psychic: Let Spirit Guide RSW read your fortune." I may have to seriously consider this. I'll need to make a living somehow because – after telling Paige I've got a spirit guide – I'll undoubtedly be jobless.

OK, just chill Annie. Remember how the old Asian saying goes: "If a problem has a solution, you have nothing to worry about. And if a problem doesn't have a solution, you have nothing to worry about." But I'm a control-obsessed Westerner, so of course, all I can do is worry. Seriously, I need to have a plan. But I also have to remember what Cathy said: Focus on the positive in the present. I'm going to focus on enjoying Liz's big day tomorrow. I'll take her daughter to see her after 15 years of being apart. I can't wait to see the look on her face.

Chapter 11

Writing a New Story

I'm *tooling my little Bug down the freeway with Liz's daughter, Natalie, beside me, trying hard not to think how I have only a few days to get myself out of this mess. One would think it was sheer insanity to have RSW "agree" to this book project, but I want to publish a book so badly.*

Better shift my mind to something more pleasant. Like what Ben is doing at this very moment. I just can't forget his kiss, his touch, his smell. My heart still speeds up when I think about him, and yet he's probably already dismissed me as "that kind of cute fat girl who turned out to be crazy." I've thought of calling him but don't have the cojones to pick up the phone. OK, maybe this isn't the best thing to obsess about either. Must focus on the now.

Liz's daughter is pretty and so serious. I still can't believe I've orchestrated this whole thing. I'll say this for Cinderella: She's prompted me to do things I would have never attempted before. But hey, Liz deserves it. Still, it's kind of uncomfortable to be in such close quarters with someone I barely know. This marathon silence has grown increasingly unbearable. Natalie hasn't said a word to me since she hopped in my car. I guess it's not easy to get picked up by a stranger to go meet your estranged mom.

As if reading my mind, Natalie speaks, softly.

"I apologize for being so quiet … this is just such a weird moment in my life. I'm sure you know that I haven't spoken to my mother in 15 years."

"Yes, I know. Liz, your mother told me."

Her intelligent brown eyes fix on my profile.

"So how do you know my mom?"

"Huh? Oh, we took a class together."

"What kind of class?"

If I tell her the truth, she'll think her mother is bonkers. She'll picture her poor crazy mom wandering down the street, dressed as Cinderella and holding a little shoe in her hand while looking to slip it on her missing daughter's foot.

"A … philosophy class."

"Philosophy? I had no idea she enjoyed that type of thing."

Maybe it's time for a subject change and to satisfy my journalistic side.

"I don't mean to meddle, but why didn't you connect with your mother sooner?"

Natalie stares out the passenger window now, watching the traffic rush by. In a small voice she starts to spill her story.

"I've thought about trying to find her because I missed her so much. I used to cry my eyes out. But I believed she should be the one looking for me. After all, she was the one who didn't support me when I needed her the most. It was very hard to leave home when I was so young and live with a man my parents didn't approve of. But I was just a kid, an immature kid who wanted to get her way no matter what the cost was. When you called me to tell me mom has been looking for me all these years, I had mixed feelings. I felt happy and confused at the same time. Why didn't she contact me earlier? She had my old address in L.A. It's not that hard finding people these days, you know. Then I found out something that really upset me. That's when I decided we needed to reconcile. It was all water under the bridge."

"What happened?"

Natalie's gentle voice is now tinged with bitterness.

"My husband told our old neighbors not to give out our address to anyone. He also refused to leave a forwarding address with the post office. When I cried because I missed my mother, he would tell me: 'She knows where to find you. It's obvious she just doesn't miss you!' Then, during one of our ugliest fights – we've had a lot – he confessed that he had thrown all of my mom's letters."

"You never opened your own mail?"

"He always managed to get the mail before I did. He always got home from work first, so he'd collect the letters from the doorman. Who knows? Maybe he threatened the poor guy. That's the kind of man he is; he can be very controlling and scary. I'm sorry, I really don't want to talk about him anymore. Right now, all I want is to see my mother."

"Wow. You've been living with that guy from Sleeping with the Enemy. Ooh, sorry. Me and my big mouth."

"You don't have to apologize. He did have a lot in common with that character. He was so full of rage. He wanted to control everyone around him. Still, in some strange way, I understand where he's coming from. My parents hurt him. Mainly Dad, who wouldn't let him in his house after he asked to marry me."

"But didn't you see he was trouble? Liz said you two had hardly dated before you wanted to get married."

Natalie sighs.

"I was pregnant. I ran away because I was afraid my parents would find out. My family lived in a small town then. People were conservative. A 19-year-old pregnant from a 40-year-old man was a scandal. I asked my mother to talk my father into letting us get married right away, but she chickened out and didn't back me up."

I find myself speaking quickly, rushing in to protect my friend.

"Liz didn't know you were pregnant. I'm sure if she would have known, everything would have turned out differently."

Natalie sighs again and stares intently at her hands, which she has folded neatly on her lap – just as I've seen her mother do a dozen times.

"Maybe. But at least now we have a chance to set things straight."

"Your mother is a very special person, Natalie. I haven't known her that long, and yet she's helped me so much."

Natalie smiles and rolls her eyes.

"Yeah, well, Mom always loved giving advice."

"We're almost there. I think it's somewhere around here."

"Oh, God, Annie. I think my heart is going to jump out of my mouth! Do you think she'll recognize me? Will she think I look OK?"

"Absolutely! You look just like her, you know. She'll probably say you need to eat more, but that's typical mom advice."

Natalie laughs.

"Do you get along with your parents?"

"My mom passed away. She was my best friend. Now, my dad – that's a different story. We haven't talked in seven years."

"Oh, I see. Annie, I realize I'm not the best person to give advice on the subject and I know I hardly know you, but please don't let any more time go by without talking to your dad. I'm so sorry I did that with my mom. It was just my stupid pride that stopped me from really looking for her. Think of all that time we lost together."

"Well, let's forget about my story. The important thing right now is to find your mother and give her a big hug. I'll drop you off. Do you need me to wait for you?"

"No, thanks. I'll take a cab. Annie, I don't know how to thank you."

"You don't need to. Truth is, I did this for me. It's been a long time since I've left my little selfish world and reached out to someone. And Liz deserves it. I really have grown to like and admire your mom."

Natalie is smiling broadly now, her face lit up like a little girl waiting for her birthday surprise.

"I can't wait to touch her and smell her lavender scent. She always smelled of lavender. My kids can't wait to meet their grandma."

I'm glancing down at the Post-it stuck to my dashboard, checking to see whether the address scrawled across it matches the house number on the tidy white cottage with green shutters.

"4834? Yes, this must be it. I'm pretty sure this is her house."

"Why are all these cars parked in front? Are you sure this is the right place?"

"Oh, wait, there's someone coming out of the house. Let's ask him. Excuse me? Sir? Is this Liz White's house?"

"Yes. Are you here for the wake?"

My stomach tightens like a clenched fist.

"A wake? There must be some kind of mistake. We're looking for Liz's house."

"That's her house, miss. Liz passed away two days ago."

The next few moments are a blur. I wrap Natalie – whose face has gone completely white – in my arms, as if to shield her from this horrible news. But it's too late. Liz is gone. We stay like this for a long time, standing in the front yard and weeping. Liz's sister, Donna, comes out on the lawn to meet us. She has Liz's eyes.

We silently follow Donna into the home, where I listen to her sandpaper voice as she explains that Liz died of heart failure. How ironic, I think. I say all the right things, nod at strangers and park myself in a corner love seat. There are no words to describe this uncomfortable mix of pain and numbness and anger. I'm sad to have to say goodbye to such a good person, but I'm also angry at the waste of it all – the years that passed while both failed to make amends. Poor Liz never got to hug her daughter one more time. Why didn't Natalie forgive her sooner? Why couldn't she find it in her heart? But what is the good in answering these questions? Liz is gone. It's too late. It doesn't matter anymore.

It's so sad to say goodbye to people we care about. I think about my own mother – dressed in her best green dress – in her casket. I recall the bottomless pain that came from realizing I would never see her gentle gray eyes again. I would never hear her ladylike chuckle or the sound of her quiet voice gently chiding me for skipping church. I gaze at the ornately framed portrait of Liz – undoubtedly taken in the '90s, when glamour shots were the rage. She is wrapped in white fur, a heavy choker of faux gems encircles her neck and her hair is teased into an elaborate bouffant. But the "Dynasty"-era trappings don't detract from her eyes – the warmest, kindest eyes I've seen. Couldn't a bad person die instead? Why couldn't Liz have lived just one more day?

Poor Natalie. She looks like a zombie – like her life has lost all meaning. I wonder why something so horrible has to happen for us to get our priorities straight. Stupid, selfish pride.

Why do we procrastinate when it comes to such precious affairs in life? But what right do I have to make judgments? I haven't spoken to my own dad in seven years. I've let my pride and anger keep me from re-connecting with the only father I've ever had. I don't want to be in Natalie's shoes. I don't want to hug him again when he's in his casket. I want to see him now. Oh, God, I miss him. What's stopping me from seeing him? I know he's not perfect. Liz wasn't perfect either. I'm not perfect. So what am I waiting for?

I say my goodbyes, give Natalie a final hug and tell her to keep in touch. "If there's anything I can do ..." I say, hating myself for murmuring such a tired, useless sentiment. *Let's face it: There is nothing I can do. I can't bring back Liz, so I'm stuck doing the ineffectual little rituals that everyone else practices at funerals – whispering clichés and bringing casseroles.*

I climb into my car, slam the door and begin to sob. The hot tears continue to pour down my face as I ride down the freeway, this time in the opposite direction. At one point, my sight is so blurred by tears that I have to pull over onto the shoulder. *What am I doing? Do I really think I can ignore my father for all these years and then just pop back into his life? Do I really want to make amends? After all these years lost, we will be like strangers. Where will we even start? And yet I can't forget that look on Natalie's face – that horrible realization she'd lost something that could never be re-captured. Liz herself told me to follow my heart. My brain is buzzing with reasons why I shouldn't do this, but my heart tells me to keep driving. I really do want to see him. I don't want it to be too late.*

I take the same familiar exit, drive the same familiar road, and turn at the same familiar street signs. I haven't been this way in years, but few things have changed. Dad lives in an older neighborhood – a place of huge trees and quaint little bungalows. As I pull in front of his house, I still want to flee. This is every bit as hard as I'd imagined – maybe even harder. I sit in my car for at least five minutes, debating whether I should just take off before he sees me. *What will he say to me? What will I say to him? What if I can't forgive him?*

And then I think of Liz's wise words: "Forgiving is not about forgetting the old story. It's about giving yourself a chance to write a new story."

We need this opportunity to forgive each other. I need to let myself choose love instead of pain. If Cinderella had left the ball a minute later, the charm would have evaporated right before the prince's eyes. Unlike Natalie, I'm not going to let that happen. I'll empower myself to write a new story. And the time to do it is now. Right now. And from now on I will forgive myself for not being able to forgive him, because for many years I thought forgiveness means to forget. Today I learned that forgiveness means giving another chance, and I will give to me and to my dad another chance.

With a shaking hand, I ring the bell. Dad opens the door, looking older and more haggard than I remembered him. But he's still wearing his favorite sweater – that ratty old cardigan he liked to wear when puttering around the house. As soon as I see that sweater, my anger melts like ice cubes in the sun. For the first time in my life, I am not consumed with what he did in the past or whether he will hurt me again. I am in the here and now, sobbing as he wraps his arms around me. I hope Liz realizes her death was not in vain. I hope she knows her daughter wanted to write a new story. I hope she knows that I'm writing a new story, too.

I hope she knows she's a real heroine. Because she had the courage to chase her dreams, even till her last breath. She's a heroine …

… for the courage to love.

… for the courage to ask for forgiveness.

… for the courage to forgive.

… for the courage to allow herself to write a new story.

… and wherever she is, I hope she knows that she did.

Chapter 12

Heroic Attitude

The last few days have been really weird. I feel this unsettling mix of grief and joy. Of course, I'm devastated by Liz's death, and the fact she and Natalie never made amends. That day for me feels like a surreal European movie that I will never forget. I worked up the nerve to call Natalie the day after Liz's wake. She still sounded very shaken, but she actually thanked me for trying to patch things up between her and her mom. "I wish I'd been big enough to do it myself," she told me. "I can never bring her back. I wasted so much time. Didn't you mention you were estranged from your dad, Annie? I hope you don't do the same with your dad."

But even as I'm grief-stricken for Liz and sorry for Natalie, I'm also happy to have reunited with Dad. He wants to spoil me rotten to make up for these last seven years. Hey, I'm not complaining. After years of blundering through life alone, I adore being spoiled by a loved one. It feels great to hear him say: "Put your coat on, honey. It's cold out there," or: "Annie, you're too skinny." Any woman loves to hear she's too skinny, even if it comes from an adoring parent who has no clue that you're still 10 pounds overweight (at least I've lost another two pounds – probably water from all the tears). That's not to say it's all been smooth sailing. It's weird when Ashley asks who I was talking to after I hang up the phone and I hear myself saying, "My dad." He hasn't been in my life for so long.

Some days I just want to turn to him and scream: "Why did you leave when I needed you most? Don't you know how you hurt me?" But then I remember Liz's words: "Forgiving is not about forgetting the old story. It's about giving yourself a chance to write a new story."

So Dad and I have attempted a few awkward conversations about the past, and we've made a little progress. We realize healing won't happen overnight, but we both seem committed to working at it.

And Hallelujah! I'm again in the association meeting room, waiting for the very last meeting. But it's so incredibly hard to see Liz's empty chair next to me.

Cathy enters the room, looking more subdued than usual. Her trademark bright suits and scarves have been replaced by a perfectly tailored black pencil skirt, white silk blouse and black pumps.

"Good evening, everyone. Before we start our last meeting, let's have a moment of silence in memory of our friend Liz, who passed away this past month. Liz has been attending association meetings for some time now, and we've always appreciated her heart and insight. She will be dearly missed."

I can't help but tear up – again. After a few moments, Cathy breaks the silence.

"Thank you. Now, we'll get to the last part of Cinderella's story."

" 'Cinderella was crying because she was feeling sad and was losing hope. At that very moment, her fairy godmother appeared. With a touch of her magic wand, she turned Cinderella's rags into a gorgeous gown and her worn-out slippers into little crystal slippers. She turned a pumpkin into a pretty carriage, led by the little house pets, which she turned into two coachmen and four beautiful horses. Cinderella jumped up and down with joy. The fairy, however, warned her: The magic will last only until midnight.

" 'Cinderella was so beautiful everyone looked at her when she entered the palace. The prince wanted to dance with her, nobody else. She almost missed her deadline so she left in a hurry and lost her crystal slipper on the staircase. She had no time to go back and pick it up.

" 'The prince was madly in love with Cinderella, so he swore he would find her himself. So after the ball he went door to door and asked every woman in the kingdom to try on the slipper. Until he knocked on Cinderella's door.

" 'The stepsisters were eager to try on the shoe, but their feet were way too big and clumsy and they couldn't jam them in the tiny crystal slipper, no matter now many times they tried.

" 'When Cinderella wanted to try it on, her stepsisters made fun of her and laughed out loud. The laughter stopped short as soon as they saw how well Cinderella's foot fit into the tiny slipper.

" 'At that very moment, her fairy godmother appeared and once again turned Cinderella's ragged clothes into a beautiful gown. The wicked stepmother and her daughters fell on their knees and asked the 'princess' of the ball for forgiveness. Cinderella gave them a big hug and forgave them with all her heart. She married the prince and they lived happily ever after.'

"There's a part in this passage that says the fairy godmother changed Cinderella's little animal friends into four beautiful horses and two coachmen and a pumpkin into a carriage. As I mentioned in one of our first meetings the word *fairy* comes from the Latin word *fata*, which means *Goddess of Destiny*. Do you remember that? This way we can justify the presence of the "fairy element" as the strength of the *Grand Life*, the power that encourages us to find our destiny. It's interesting to notice the potential for transformation of the *Grand Life*."

True to form, Steve is the first to speak.

"What do you mean by potential for transformation, Cathy?"

"Steve, in nature everything is changeable and in constant motion. This is what happens when we walk with the *Grand Life*. When Cinderella talked to her little animal friends, she would have never imagined that they would be changed into coachmen and beautiful horses. She would never have imagined that a simple pumpkin would turn into a pretty carriage."

"I'm sure no one could imagine that. It's impossible for that to happen in real life anyway."

"Steve, as I've been saying all along, we're gathered here to interpret the symbolism of this story and this passage reveals something to us that is very important for our life."

"What's that?"

"I interpret this passage as a revelation of the power of the *Grand Life* to change things and that everything that happens to us happens for a reason, even though sometimes we're unable to recognize it."

"What do you mean?"

It's Beatrice this time.

"Well, Cinderella's sisters probably thought: "What kind of fool befriends filthy, little rodents? They're good for nothing." Or Cinderella herself could have thought: "I am alone here with these animals that are nothing but pests. Life isn't *fair*. However, at the end of the story, destiny changed these tiny creatures into important elements in Cinderella's story. They actually helped her achieve her dream. When we trust in the *Grand Life's* power to guide our lives, we know that where we are now and who we are with is exactly where we need to be. Sometimes we believe that an outstanding person with good contacts can help us. But life will surprise you, and you'll get help from the person you least expected."

Cathy certainly has a point. For instance, I never thought my employer would be the one helping me publish my book. Well, not my book, but RSW's book. Sometimes the opportunity for transformation is closer than we think.

"Look, Cathy, I realize I'm probably the most annoying person in this group."

Cathy nods at Steve, smiling in reply to his lopsided grin. I'm beginning to wonder why Steve keeps coming to these classes if he has so many issues with them. Wow, talk about a paradigm shift. I've gone from thinking Steve was one of the only smart people in the room to being irritated by his constant skepticism.

"Well, I'm going to test your patience again. Truth is, it bothers me to hear these explanations based on fairy tales and passages from the Bible. I'd like to get examples closer to reality – examples that hit closer to home, you know what I mean?"

"Absolutely, Steve. And please, don't think you're annoying. You are probably one of the most curious ones in class, and curiosity can be a valuable thing. Let me tell you a story about a boy named Walter Elias. Walter came from a poor family and his father was strict. He loved to draw farm animals and considered them his friends. Like Cinderella, he spent hours talking to them. If there was no scrap paper at home, Walter would draw on wrapping paper.

"Every time his father caught him sitting or talking with the pigs, the ducks or the chickens, he would tell him to do something more worthwhile instead. After hearing this story, many might think: "Poor kid. He's all alone, talking to the animals." That little boy later turned out to be one of the most-famous people of the 20th century: Walt Disney. So let me ask you a question: Would he be who he turned out to be had he not gone through all these experiences? Didn't the *Grand Life* have a purpose when it guided him to spend time with the animals? When I think about his fantastic creations such as Mickey Mouse and Donald Duck, I have no doubt in my mind that the *Grand Life* had a wonderful purpose for this 'poor' young boy."

"That's a good example. But do you believe that during those hard times Walt Disney was aware that everything he was going through had some grand purpose?"

Is that the sound of hell freezing over? Steve actually decides to be generous at our last meeting. Better late than never, I suppose.

"No one can answer that, Steve. Everything I talk about here is the product of my own interpretations. But I can tell you what Walt Disney said in one of his biographies. "All the hardship, troubles and hurdles I went through made me only stronger. I didn't need a pillow or a large bed with silk sheets to be happy. It didn't bother me where I ate – everything was an experience."

"I like that example better. But you know, I am an artist by nature but work as an accountant, and when I am the only one to see all my paintings in my closet it gets really frustrating. Walt Disney was a person who was successful in life anyway and his socioeconomic level isn't remotely close to mine. Do you have an example that hits closer to home?"

"Steve, many people say it's difficult to make money doing what they love. Many artists find it impossible to live off of their art so they give up their dreams in the middle of their careers. When we look at brilliant careers – such as that of Brazilian painter Romero Britto, who is internationally recognized as one of the greatest representatives of pop art – we can't even begin to imagine the heroic life that's behind the great achievements."

"I don't know his story although I admire his art very much. Of course, I could never afford to buy one of his paintings, but I could recognize his work anywhere."

"I can assure you that in the beginning of his career, Romero did not have the means to live an exciting life. He was the son of a modest family from the state of Pernambuco, a very remote area of Brazil. As a child, Romero painted on the walls of his house. He dreamed of doing his art while traveling around the world. He saved some money and was able to go to Miami to sell his paintings on the street. Imagine if you would have passed and seen one of his paintings. Would it ever cross your mind that this guy – this street artist – would become a world-renowned painter? But the *Grand Life* has a reason for everything, even the hard times. If we're giving life our best, it's only a matter of time before we recognize that reason. In Romero's case, it's obvious that by displaying his paintings on the street, he increased the chances of someone important walking by and admiring his art. When we do our best and trust in the *Grand Life*, we start to see that in life there are no coincidences, there is just providence."

Steve is actually nodding and smiling.

"That example may have convinced me, Cathy."

She continues ...

"The reason I'm giving you all these stories is to show that we can practice a heroic attitude only when we understand that everything happens for a reason. There's even a reason why we go through hard times: to develop our potential and to find absolute fulfillment."

Beatrice asks a question.

"And what was Cinderella's heroic attitude, Cathy?"

"Naturally, it showed itself when, after all the cruelty and stinginess that her stepmother and stepsisters had shown to her, Cinderella still found it in her heart to forgive. At that moment she proved to be a real heroine. Trust me, only heroes are capable of doing that. I know executives who are able to direct large companies and have a good relationship with thousands of employees, but they lack the ability to forgive anyone. It's not because that's how they want to live. Nobody wants to have a heart filled with sorrow. You can't feel fulfilled and successful when you are dogged by a series of unsuccessful relationships.

"Webster defines the word *forgive* as to *absolve from guilt. Guilt* means *responsibility*. So whenever we say we *forgive* someone, we're saying that we believe that person to be responsible for our pain and that by our 'divine goodness' we're going to forgive him. If you understand this, then in order to forgive we have to have judged the other person and declared him guilty – i.e., responsible for our unhappiness. Only then can we decide whether we want to pardon him."

There are nods around the class; even Steve and Beatrice seem to be impressed.

"We have to understand that there's a reason behind everything that happens to us and that the *Grand Life's* goal is to encourage us to attain fulfillment. Only then can we avoid blaming other people or circumstances for our unhappiness and see in them an opportunity to grow. It's very dangerous to place the responsibility for our happiness on other people or circumstances. What if Walt Disney would have accused his father of being too tough on him and used that as an excuse to be a shiftless drifter for the rest of his life? Don't you think maybe his father's attitude made him seek refuge in the animals and thus inspired him to create his stories? We consider Cinderella a humble and kind young woman because of her noble attitude. She was kind to her stepmother and sisters even though they treated her horribly.

We can identify the strength and splendor of the light only in the face of darkness."

Beatrice's brow is furrowed.

"What? So it's better to not forgive? Now I'm confused."

"What I am trying to illustrate is that we declare someone guilty before we forgive him. When we understand that there's a reason behind everything, we stop judging and free ourselves from guilt. Where there is no guilt there is no judgment; where there is no judgment there is no need for forgiveness. You don't need to carry the weight of deciding whether you forgive the other person. By the law of action and reaction, each person offers what he or she has to offer and receives what he or she gives in return. If there's someone we need to forgive, to free from guilt, it's ourselves. Instead of worrying about who we have to forgive, we need to start by forgiving ourselves. Then we can free ourselves from the weight of judging others and thus allow ourselves to see the *Grand Life's* grand purpose."

Uh oh, Steve looks distressed.

"But, Cathy, some people hurt us so terribly that it's hard to forget what they did to us. You'd have to be a saint."

"That's why I left that teaching for last, Steve. We can understand the teaching about forgiveness after we go over the other teachings. When we get hurt by someone, it's usually because he or she did something that didn't meet our expectations of them, right?"

"Right."

"If we create expectations in regards to someone else's attitude, it's because somehow we're trying to control the future. When we behave that way, we allow the negative voices to start saying things such as: 'How could he do that to me? I didn't deserve to be treated that way.' What we're really saying is: 'I didn't want that to happen to me.' When we do our best and treat others with respect and generosity, we don't complain when what we don't want to happen happens. Instead, we behave like heroes and heroines by remembering that what happens in life is not what we want to happen but what needs to happen in order for us to achieve our dreams."

I have a question.

"What's the best way to behave during these moments?"

"Instead of accusing the other person or the circumstance and placing the responsibility for your unhappiness in someone else's hands, we should take responsibility and ask ourselves: 'What can I learn from this? How can this help me become a better person?' I believe that people who don't take responsibility for their pain and sadness cannot take responsibility for their success and joy."

"Cathy, even you have to admit it's not easy to think that way."

"Indeed. It's not easy to be a heroine, Beatrice. But it becomes easier once we start using our magic wand, that little wand that has the power to turn a pumpkin into a beautiful carriage and old rags into a beautiful dress."

"What magic wand is that?"

I have to ask this question myself. See? I'm living in the present! Not as many wandering thoughts into the past or the future anymore.

"Annie, that magic wand is love. It's the practice of true, pure, unconditional love. It's useless to love a rose and say you don't want to put up with its thorns. To really love a rose is to also love its thorns. Many people get upset when they read "and they lived happily ever after," because they think it's Utopia."

"Yes, that's right, Cathy. Nobody can be happy forever and ever. That's stuff for sugar-and-honey fairy tales."

"Steve, only when we become responsible for our own happiness can we truly be happy forever. You can't be truly happy when you put the burden of your happiness in someone else's hands. I truly believe that it is not the things that happen to us but how we choose to react to them that define happiness. We can react to a situation with happiness or sadness. It's our choice."

I have to throw in my two cents.

"But Cathy, what you're telling us isn't logical. There are times in our lives when people or circumstances hurt us tremendously and we feel a deep pain that won't go away."

"I'm saying that we can choose to react happily to the pain."

Steve is getting worked up again.

"Are you kidding? But that's impossible!"

"Steve, ask any mom who has given birth and she will say that while she was feeling the pains of giving birth, she felt happiness in her heart. And there's only one way to handle that: by practicing real love. When we understand that, no matter how painful it is, there's a higher purpose for everything that happens in our lives. It's the higher purpose of making us grow and helping us find our way. We have the power to decide to deal with life's situations with happiness – the happiness of knowing that we are facing an opportunity to grow. The happiness of knowing that we're going to have the opportunity to choose whether we're going to behave like heroes or like mere mortals, full of self-pity and complaints."

"I'm having trouble wrapping my brain around all this. What do you consider *true love*?"

"It's the love that frees us from fear and guilt. It's the love that allows us to be happy, regardless of our circumstances. It's the love that loves the Cinderella in us – our kind, humble, hardworking side. It's the love that loves the stepmother in us – the side that wants to oppress our hero. And this dark side gives us a chance to express the light in us. We have a chance to show our courage when we're afraid. We have the chance to express our faith when we have doubts. We have the chance to express our love when we feel hurt by someone."

Absolute silence in the room. It's like we're all actors in an old-fashioned murder mystery, gathered in the drawing room to find out who killed the leading lady. I'm actually going to miss these meetings. I haven't always understood them, but they've helped me a lot. Looks like I've become indoctrinated. Another card-carrying member of the Cinderella cult. Intent on getting in the last word, Steve stands up.

"Cathy, I realize we're running out of time, but this story of forgiveness is still confusing to me. If I love even the tough things that happen to me, then I end up not accusing anybody and, consequently, I don't feel hurt or the need to forgive. I can even choose to react happily to these situations, right? It sounds like preventive 'life medicine.' But do you really expect us to be able to forget what people have done to hurt us? After all, we're only human. Didn't God give us a memory so we wouldn't open ourselves up to the same toxic people or to making the same painful mistakes?"

As if it has a mind of its own, my right hand shoots into the air. Cathy smiles at me and nods.

"Yes, Annie?"

"It's something Liz told me. I'll never forget what she said to me once when I was having an especially bad day. She said 'to forgive is not to forget the old story, but to give yourself a chance to write a new one.' "

Cathy fixes the class with a radiant smile.

"Thank you so much for sharing that, Annie. You've helped us end this last meeting with wise words from such a beloved person. I think it's amazing that, even though her death is painful and we all miss her, Liz still found a way to touch our lives and help us.

"And with that one perfect thought, this is pretty much the end. I hope these meetings helped motivate you to achieve your fulfillment. So if I must try to wrap up these past five lessons in a nutshell, I will tell you these things:

Cathy reveals the board, and her steady hand fills the white space.

- *Allow yourselves to give life your best.*
- *Remember that you and your story have value. Love the flowers and the thorns in your life.*
- *Empower yourselves to work hard to make your dreams come true. Allow yourselves to trust.*
- *Allow yourselves to fall and to get back up.*
- *Allow yourselves to succeed and to make mistakes.*
- *Allow yourselves to truly love.*

"I hope you all go back home and allow yourself to write a new story. A story of heroes and heroines. A story of men and women of extraordinary value. A story in which you will indeed live happily ever after."

Chapter 13

And They Lived Happily Ever After

After the last meeting, I sort through everything that has happened in the last few months. My life really has improved although I still have a ways to go. I'm excited to be writing a new story with my dad. When I look at myself in the mirror, I'm relatively happy with my body – not because I'm on some insane diet program, but because I've grown to respect the place where my soul and spirit live. One of the best things I've ever done for myself is to transform my pessimistic "inner stepmother" into a more nurturing voice and trusting that the best will happen in my life. I'd like to say I'll never feel depressed or start undervaluing myself again, but I can't guarantee that. But rather than dwell on what the future might bring, I try to live in the moment. All I know is that I was able to do something that once seemed impossible: write a new story with my dad. And if I can do that, I should be able to write a new story for myself.

Needless to say, I'd love to end my story kissing Prince Charming while romantic music swells in the background and a cherub flutters by with a "They lived happily ever after" sign. Well, things don't always turn out the way we planned. At least now, with my new skills, I have learned to accept things the way they are, instead of agonizing over how I'd like them to be. Maybe this is the way things are supposed to be right now. Maybe the "Grand Life" has another wonderful man in store for me.

So now I'm in one of the chrome-and-glass elevators at the Clarkson Building, heading up to Women & Co.'s editorial offices on the 36th floor. My mission is to participate in a meeting with Jack Weber, one of the country's most influential publishers. After having sorted through two million evil plans to get myself out of this dilemma, I've decided to do what's right and tell the truth. I'm aware I might lose my job and my dream of publishing my book might not happen (at least with a major publishing house), but I'd rather take a risk than go on living a lie. I'm not going to think about anything else. I'm just going to walk into Paige's office and tell the truth. I refuse to entertain any negative thoughts. Instead, I will live in the moment and trust that the "Grand Life" will give me the courage to fulfill my dream.

OK, what's going on? Why are so many people heading toward Paige's office? Ohmigod, it feels like everyone in the editorial department is going to be in this meeting. This is insane! If I make my big confession in front of all these people, there's going to be a lynch mob. Chill, Annie Joseph – stop thinking! Just go to the meeting, do your best and trust in the "Grand Life." Remember: You are not alone.

Paige is there, looking tres chic in a Chloe tweed jacket with cropped silk trousers. She radiates excitement.

"Annie! I'm so glad you made it!"

As if I had any choice.

"We're including most of the editors and senior writers in this exciting announcement. Everyone's so thrilled to finally meet RSW! I don't know whether you've met Laura, our book editor? And of course Jack Weber, the fabulous publisher of Weber & Howard Publishing? So dear, where is RSW? You said she was coming with you."

"RSW's here, Paige."

"Here? Where, darling?"

"In this room."

"Annie, please!"

Paige mutters under her breath, and then adds, sharply.

"Is RSW a ghost? Are you her medium?"

My reply is loud and clear.

"No, Ashley, RSW is not a ghost."

Paige is glaring at me now, irritated that I'm embarrassing her in front of a roomful of important people.

"OK, then where is she? Could you be more specific?"

"Paige, I don't know how to tell you this. I-I'm RSW."

"What?"

Her face has gone white beneath her perfectly applied foundation.

"What do you mean, you are RSW?"

"I'm sorry, Paige. I owe you an explanation."

I tell them everything, from the first meeting with Paige to the "birth" of RSW. Along the way, I tell them about my journey with the Cinderella workshop and all the changes in my life. Normally, I would feel self-conscious with so many people staring at me and would stammer and stumble. But for once, I am focused and articulate. The words flow out of me with ease. After I'm done speaking my piece, I am greeted by silence. Silence you couldn't slice through with a buzz saw. And so I take another deep breath, and just keep going.

"You see, when Paige read my first RSW article, I still wasn't appreciative of my sensitive side – that side that's not afraid to talk about dreams, anxieties and fears. All my life, I've always been strong, and strong for me meant covering up my human side – what I thought of as my 'weaknesses' – beneath a mask. Now I know that being strong means acknowledging and accepting your human side, including your vulnerabilities. That's why I'm asking you to please forgive me. And to forgive, I learned in these meetings, is not to forget what I did but to give me a chance to show what I can do."

A familiar, well-bred voice cuts through the silence in the room. It's Gabrielle.

"So this supposed RSW, including her "social phobia," was basically a ruse?"

"Actually, Gabrielle, that part is true. That extremely sensitive side of me, RSW, was hidden. I was afraid to show it. When I began to practice true love – the love that embraces light and darkness, pain and happiness – I decided to love myself wholly and unconditionally, not just one part of me. It was then that I gathered the courage to accept the "RSW" in me. Now I'm ready to admit that I indeed am RSW, and I wrote those things. So in a way, love healed my, or RSW's, social phobia. Love set me free."

The silence has become unbearable. I cannot read the look on Paige's face. Finally, she speaks, and her tone is icy-cold.

"Well, understandably, this is quite a surprise. Staff: Please return to work with the understanding that this information should not leave this office. Naturally, if our competitors caught wind that RSW is an invention, well, it could be quite embarrassing for all of us. Annie? Would you please wait in my conference room? Naturally, I will need to decide what action to take, and I have things to discuss with Jack."

Paige's smirking assistant ushers me into the adjoining conference room – a posh space with sleek Danish furnishings and floor-to-ceiling windows overlooking the city. As she closes the door behind her, I am surprised by how calm I feel. I am almost certain to be fired. I know this is the hallowed room where Paige conducts her most delicate business: whether it be meeting with important dignitaries or working out severance packages with soon-to-be- terminated employees. There is a side door that leads to a back hallway, which leads to a personal elevator. All the better for security to discretely lead out a sobbing, ranting ex-employee, I suspect.

There is a time when the prospect of termination would have left me sobbing and pleading with the best of them. But I feel serene. I know I did the right thing in telling the truth. I know I am a strong, talented, hardworking woman. And I know that this whole merry-go-round had to happen for a reason – even if it means unemployment. But who says it will? I refuse to assume the worst will happen. I will embrace whatever comes my way. And whatever it is, I will feel blessed. After all, this whole experience has helped me grow so much. I've made new breakthroughs, stopped living in fear and discovered a self-possession I never knew I had. The "Grand Life" almost certainly has great things in store for me. And so I don't need to panic or live with regret. And so I'll just stand here, taking in the city skyline.

I hear the door open, followed by Paige's well-modulated voice.

"Annie?"

I turn to sit down at the table.

"I really must apologize for breaking all this to you in that meeting. I have to add that I just appreciate all the opportunities I've received at *Women & Co.* I really am grateful for what you've done for me, and I want you to know that I think you run a fine publication. At the same time, I want to emphasize that I really have worked hard and contributed much to *Women & Co.* For years, it has been my life."

"Who said you're going to be fired?"

"I'm not? I'm a bit confused."

Paige holds up a hand, smiling.

"To be honest, when you were telling your whole story, I was livid. I really did want to fire you. I couldn't believe all the conversations we'd had about RSW – all the opportunities you'd had to tell me she wasn't real. I was so shocked by your deception, especially in front of someone like Jack Weber. I mean, what would he think if one of my own employees could fool me like this? And who would think such an employee would be you? Annie, you've always been so reliable – such a workhorse. Your work was never sexy, but it was always concise, clear and accurate. You seemed like such an ethical person. I was just so surprised."

"But I have always tried to be ethical, Paige. At the time, I just wasn't secure enough to admit something so personal was mine. And before I knew it, the whole thing had gotten out of hand."

"Of course, then I realized RSW isn't a lie at all. As you said, RSW is your purest truth, your reality. She is nothing more than a pseudonym for you – a writer with more insight than we knew you possessed. A writer who has a lot to say."

"Well, thank you."

"And when I really calmed down a bit and thought about it, I actually felt some admiration for what you'd just done. Of course, I didn't appreciate the ruse."

Paige pauses, and her smile grows steely as she fixes me with an unblinking gaze.

"But to be perfectly honest, Annie, we would be fools to fire you. Why should we let *Bliss* magazine snatch you up? Jack and I were talking, and you're going to make us a lot of money"

A-ha! So the real Paige finally reveals herself. I should have realized a tough bird like her could talk ad nauseum about "sensitivity" and "inner truth," but would never lose sight of the bottom line.

"But how are we going to tell the readers, Paige? Or are we going to keep it quiet? I really don't want to continue with this charade."

"Who said we're going to keep quiet? This will allow you to write your investigative piece as a transformational, first-person piece and to contribute the next entry for a special edition of *Everyday Heroines.* Could you imagine a more heroic story than yours? We're also going to discuss publishing RS ... I mean, your book with Jack. But before all that, I have one question that I absolutely must ask."

Amazed that I haven't already been bundled off to ride the Back Elevator of Shame, I'm smiling ear to ear.

"Yes?"

"The acronym RSW. You must tell me. What does it mean?

Annie Joseph, think fast, you can't say that means Really Stupid Woman...

"It means, it means, Really Splendid Woman!"

The meeting with Jack Weber goes extremely well. They decide to kick off my book – a collection of my short stories intermingled with RSW columns that reinforce the themes of the stories – with a nationwide book signing and all the perks. They also want to follow it up with a collection of "Annie 'RSW' Joseph's Empower Yourself" pieces. Today, I feel like a heroine.

It's almost the end of one of the best days of my life, and I'm stationed at my desk, hammering out my special contribution to Everyday Heroines. I know, I know. I used to loathe this column. But love works magic in our lives. It has the power to transform. So I love this column now, and I love the inspiration it gives to aspiring Cinderellas out there. And you know what? I miss my prince. Maybe I should call Ben. I don't know. It felt so good to call Dad and share the good news with him. He was as excited as if he'd received a publishing contract himself. "My Annie," he'd said. "I always knew you would do great things even when you were little. You wrote the best book reports of any 9-year-old I'd ever met." Uh-oh, hold that thought; here comes Ashley, who I'd managed to avoid until now. And she looks like she just won the lottery.

"Annie! I must be the luckiest intern in the whole department! All the other interns are sooo jealous! Everyone wants to know exactly what it's like working next to the "real RSW." I can't believe you kept this secret from me all this time. You know, your story would make an awesome book. Guess I didn't give you enough credit. You're more amazing than I thought."

"Thank you, Ashley. You're special to me too."

You know what? I actually mean it. I've grown to like Ashley, in all her ambitious, overachieving glory. Once again, Cinderella manages to work miracles.

Ashley is bent over the file cabinet, trying to cram one more manila folder into the overstuffed drawer.

"You know, I'm glad I told Ben that he didn't deserve you and you were way too good for him. At the time, I didn't really believe it, but now I see I was right. I don't know why I never figured out you were RSW."

Good Lord. I can't be hearing this correctly.

"What? What are you talking about? You spoke to Ben about me? Why on earth did you do that? And for god's sake, when?"

Ashley looks nonplussed.

"Remember the week after Gabrielle's wedding? You asked me not to mention him again. He called you that same day. I answered the phone and told him that he didn't deserve you."

I am fighting the urge to wrap my hands and around her skinny throat.

"And?"

"He asked me whether I had your new cell number."

"And what?! Tell me. Just tell me, Ashley!"

"And I told him I couldn't give it to him because you didn't want to hear from him ever again. Oh, and that you were way too good for him."

I'm fighting for composure now. No jury would convict me. Any person who had to share a cubicle with Ashley as long as I have would understand. It's justifiable homicide.

"Please, Ashley, tell me you didn't say that. Why didn't you tell me he called?"

Slowly realizing her error, Ashley's voice has taken on a defensive tone.

"You made me swear that I'd never talk to you about him ever again, remember?"

I breathe deeply and start counting to 10. By the time I reach "5," I'm capable of speaking in a semi-normal voice again.

"Ashley, I just didn't want you to tell me about his other women."

"Annie, where are you going?"

"I'm leaving. I need to give someone my new number."

As soon as I'm home, I call Ben. OK, so I'm lying again. I actually call him on my way home. I can't wait! It's so wonderful to hear his voice again, and he seems happy to hear from me. I invite him to come over that evening to talk. Deep down, I am terrified he's moved on to someone else or has decided I'm way too flaky for him. Still, I gather all my courage and quickly shut down those negative internal voices. Those voices have ruled my life for too long, and they've gotten me nowhere.

So now I'm in my apartment, waiting for Ben to arrive. The doorman has just buzzed to tell me "a gentleman" is on his way up to see me. My heart is beating so fast I fear it might explode. Can a perfectly healthy, 30-something woman die of anticipation? I had left the door cracked open, just a bit, so he can walk right in. My God! The sound of the elevator is music to my ears. I can hear his footsteps. What should I say? Should I try to explain? Should I just say hi? Will he be interested in picking up where we left off?

He walks in, looking as gorgeous as ever in charcoal-gray slacks and a chocolate suede jacket. I'm standing there in my apron, with his favorite meal – pasta with tomato sauce and basil – waiting on the table. He looks at me and starts to laugh.

I feel a tremendous release – as if I can breathe again. I had been frozen with fear – fear that he would yell at me, fear that he would call me crazy, fear that he would turn around and run. But instead he laughs – that wonderful, infectious, one-of-a-kind chuckle. I start to laugh too.

The ice broken, he shyly hands over a medium-sized package.

"What's this? You didn't need to bring anything."

He just smiles and says I should open the gift after dinner.

Before we begin to eat I slip the Michael Bolton disc into my CD player. The strains of "When a Man Loves a Woman" fill my cramped living room, and we dance, cheek-to-cheek around the beat-up coffee table. Love is the magic wand we all have in our hands. It's able to accomplish magic truths. Love turned a song I thought was tacky into the theme of my love story. We kiss – an intense kiss – a kiss of hope for the many moments we'll spend together – a kiss of love – a kiss of desire – an unforgettable kiss.

At that magic moment, I saw a neon sign light up in my head. "And they lived happily ever after ..."

After. Who knows what is going to happen after, and who told us that we need to know? I want to breathe in life today and take in each moment as it passes. Because:

FROM NOW ON I EMPOWER MYSELF ...

... TO DANCE TO THE UNKNOWN.

Ah, I nearly forgot: Just in case you're wondering, the package Ben gave me contained "passion fruit," several pieces of very juicy, perfectly ripe passion fruit.

P.S. *About RSW's next piece, could you do me a favor? I'd love to write it, but "unfortunately" I'm a little busy right now. You've followed all the association's meetings; you've watched the drama of my life, so could you do me a favor? In the next chapter could you write the article for me? I'll give you the first sentence ...*

Chapter 14

From now on, I empower myself …

You have in your hands more than a book, a password to a new world...

Go to the website www.chrislinnares.com type the password KT9185 and you can become part of the special Reader's Community.

A wonderful opportunity to exchange ideas with other readers, talk direct with Chris Linnares , and be connected with a world of people that don't live a fairy tale but they all deserve a happy ending.

Welcome!